I0683277

ReGina Crawford

Food From The Heart

Published by True Mediations of the Heart

A Division of G Styl Productions Incorporated

She changes into the bathing suit and returns to the sitting area. Quentin emerges from the bedroom on the right in a bathing suit of his own, if you could call the skimpy piece of material he was wearing a suit. "Wonderful, you're ready," he states as he enters the sitting area. He leads her to the Jacuzzi, helps her down the steps, and settles her into one of the seats. The jet sprays of warm water caress her body and massage away the day's fatigue.

As the tension in her body fades away, she looks at Quentin sitting across from her and smiles. "This is just what I needed, and I would never have done this myself. Thank you."

"You are quite welcome. It is my pleasure to serve you, just tell me what you need or desire."

"Well I remember something about a body rub."

"If that's what you want, that's what you will get." He reaches behind him for a bottle of scented body oil before scooting closer to her. He begins with her feet, then her legs and thighs. When he's ready to do her back, he holds out his hand to her, and she gladly places her hand in his. He pulls her towards him and turns her around before going to work on her neck, shoulders, and back.

True Meditations of the Heart
3232 W. 44th Street
Cleveland, OH 44109
www.Author.GStyl.com

First published on 3/15/2009.

ISBN: 978-0-615-27912-1

Printed in the United States of America.

About the Author:
ReGina is a 41 year old divorced mother of three children 2 girls and 1 boy, ages 18, 14, and 3. She has been writing since the age of ten; beginning with poetry and short stories. Her first book, a romance novella, Triple Threat, hit the market in June 2008, and the response was overwhelmingly positive. Food From The Heart is the second book in the series about the McNair's and their friends. She has had poetry published in five National Library of Poetry publications, and performs her poetry live weekly at an open mic in Cleveland, OH. She has also performed as the feature poet at other open mics in Cleveland and Columbus, OH, and her poetry can be heard on Blog Talk Radio on Saturday evenings on the show Wordplay Parley. She currently is a contributing writer to the Oldest Black Newspaper in Ohio - The Call and Post - and has been writing for the publication since September 2002. She has also had a story published in 5 Star Magazine. You can check her out on the world wide web at Author.GStyl.com, MySpace.com/GStyl, MySpace.com/GStylPoet, and GStyl.com.

Cover Design by Frost Byte Graphics, Cleveland, OH
GrafixFrost@chiefrocka.com or MySpace.com/Kingpinism

Food From The Heart

Prologue

Indigo, Jade, Ebony, and Quintana are going over the menu for the reception when Indigo's brother Quentin walks in the door. Quentin's eyes are instantly drawn to the lady sitting with his sister. Quintana looks up and her eyes lock with the most incredible light brown eyes she's ever seen, and the jolt of electricity that runs through her body leaves her breathless. Indigo, Jade, and Ebony sit back and watch the exchange for a few minutes before Indigo interrupts them. "Hello Q. Care to shut the door?"

"Huh", responds a distracted Quentin. "Oh, sorry," he states as he turns to close the door. "Hello everybody," he says after closing the door. He tries not to look in the ladies' direction knowing he wouldn't be able to control his reaction to the beautiful stranger. Quintana follows Quentin with her eyes until he leaves the room, and enters the kitchen. There are trays of food on the counter, and Quentin decides to sample some of the food. He picks up what appears to be a mini egg roll and soon discovers that it's some kind of dessert item, and it's heavenly. He samples some of the other items before leaving the kitchen. "Who made the food in the kitchen? It's wonderful."

"That would be me," Quintana states as she stands and offers Quentin her hand. "Quintana Richardson of Quintana's Restaurant and Catering."

"Beautiful, intriguing, and talented," Q half whispers. "Quentin McNair of single and interested," he states while clasping her hand in his. Both become instantly hot from the contact of their flesh.

"Nice to meet you, and I'll keep that in mind."

"You do that, since I'm sure we'll be seeing a lot of each other if you're catering the wedding." He smiles revealing the dimple in his right cheek before heading for the guest bedroom.

"Who is that," Quintana asks while resuming her seat.

"That would be my brother," states Indigo. "And from the looks of it, you two will be getting to know each other better."

"Hmm. Now that sounds like a plan," states Quintana while gathering her things together. "I'll see you ladies in a couple of days," she finishes as she heads out the door.

The ladies head for Quentin's room. They fling the door open, and find him standing there in nothing but a towel apparently daydreaming. Once he acknowledges their presence, the questions begin. "What the hell was that all about back there," asks Indigo.

"Where did you find her," asks Quentin at the same time.

"I'm the oldest here and this is my house, so my questions get answered first," responds Indigo.

"I hate it when you pull rank," he states. At her glare, he holds out his hands, "All right. I don't know what that was. I walked in the door, and I could just feel her. When I looked into her eyes, I felt mesmerized. I couldn't look away, and then when I touched her my body temp when up about twenty degrees. No one has ever affected me like that, especially not on an initial meeting."

Food From The Heart

"Sounds like someone just found their soul mate," quips Jade.

"Very funny cousin. Anyway, Sis where did you find her?"

"She's a cousin to one of the officer's wife, and Kyle thought that we should give her first shot at catering the reception. She's an excellent cook, reasonably priced, and has a good disposition. I think we'll probably use her, but we'll know for sure after having dinner at her restaurant on Friday."

"Who's having dinner at her restaurant?"

"Kyle, Keith, Kendrick, Jade, Ebony, and myself."

"Don't you think I should come along as an important member of this family, and the wedding party?"

"If you must, you can join us. I'll just go call the restaurant and change the reservation from six to seven."

Jade merely laughs as she follows Indigo and Ebony out of the room. "The boy has got it bad," states Jade. Indigo merely shakes her head as she heads for the phone. "You know you want to laugh. I don't know why you're holding it in." Indigo begins to laugh. "See I told you." Indigo has to put the phone down until she finishes laughing before she can call the restaurant.

Friday arrives, and everyone is waiting on Quentin to finish dressing. He finally emerges fifteen minutes past the time he was supposed to be ready. "Boy what took you so long," asks Indigo as he stops and turns in front of her.

"I had to put together just the right outfit," he replies. "So what do you think?"

"I think she's probably going to be too busy to notice what you are wearing."

"That's why I had to put together the right outfit, one that would make her stop and notice," he answers with a grin.

"We've wasted enough time. Let's go," states Indigo.

Quentin decides that he'll drive his own car so that he doesn't get wrinkled, and he doesn't want to feel like a fifth wheel. "Whatever," states Indigo as she gets in the front of Kyle's car.

Food From The Heart

The Prelude

They arrive at the restaurant on time, but there is a crowd in the entryway. However, they are not forced to wait the forty-five minutes that everyone else has to wait once they give their names. They have a table reserved for them in the center of the restaurant.

"Well I, for one, am glad we didn't have to wait, I'm starving," states Indigo as they are lead to their table.

"I'm glad too. I would have hated to have gotten wrinkled in that crowd," states Quentin.

"Boy, shut up and sit down," respond Indigo and Jade at the same time.

Just as everyone is seated, Quintana arrives at their table to greet them. She informs them that they can look at the menu, but that she has prepared a series of special dishes for them to try, at which point she looks directly at Quentin. He grins like a child at Christmas, and Indigo just shakes her head.

"Hello Quentin. I'm glad you could make it as well," states Quintana. Then to the table at large she states, "Someone will be with you shortly to take your drink orders, and your food should be ready in twenty minutes. I'll be back to check on you later." She heads back to the kitchen and Quentin's eyes follow her all the way there.

"Wrap up your tongue and stick it back in your mouth," whispers Indigo to her brother. His head snaps around quickly as he is drawn away from the fantasy he was indulging in after watching the sway of Quintana's hips as she walked away from the table.

"I can't believe I'm acting like this. She is just a woman, a very sexy woman, but a woman just the same," Quentin whispers to himself. However, everyone at the table hears him.

"Well then pull yourself together, and quit acting like some love sick school boy," teases Jade.

Their waiter arrives and takes their drink order. When he returns with the drinks, he also brings them each salads which are all different. Each bowl has the name of the salad on it, and they pass the bowls amongst themselves so that they can taste everyone. Quintana comes by to see which of the salads they preferred. Indigo and Keith preferred the Almond Mandarin salad, while Jade and Kyle preferred the Apple Avocado salad, and Ebony and Kendrick preferred the Asparagus and Tomato salad. Quentin couldn't make up his mind between the Lemon Zucchini Cucumber salad and the Spinach Strawberry salad. Quintana makes note of their preferences before returning to the kitchen.

A short while later their dinners arrive. A plate of Apricot Round Steak is placed in front of Kyle. Keith receives a Red Wine Vinaigrette and Cilantro Brisket, while Indigo receives Alaskan Salmon Bake with a Pecan Crunch Coating. Jade's dinner consists of Apricot-Glazed Shrimp. Ebony's dinner is Amaretto Shrimp Almandine, and Kendrick's dinner is Braised Lamb with a Sour Orange Marinade. And last but not least, Quentin is served Scallops with an Oyster and Red Pepper Sauce. Again they pass their plates around the table so that everyone has a taste of everything served. They are amazed at how wonderful everything tastes, and the variety of the flavors they are experiencing. Once again Quintana returns to their table to see what their reactions are to the food they were served. "Girl, you are definitely a danger to my waistline," states Indigo while placing her fork back on the table.

"I'm worried about more than my waistline around you," half whispers Quentin. Quintana turns in his direction, and he turns on that smile of his that reveals his lone dimple. "What can I say, you are a danger to my total well being. But I think I'm up for the challenge, are you?"

She shakes her head at him while smiling before turning back to the rest of them. She makes notes of their preferences for the different foods served. However, before heading back to the kitchen, she makes one more note and hands it to Quentin.

I close at 10:00 PM. My staff is usually out by
11:00 PM. Why don't you stop back around then?

Quentin smiles, places the note in his pocket, and then joins the conversation going on around him. The couples are discussing which dance club they should go to after leaving the restaurant. Quentin declines the invitation to go with them, saying he has another engagement to attend this evening. He tanks them for dinner, then gets up and heads for the kitchen. No one at the table says a word for a few minutes, then Kyle speaks up. "Am I missing something here? Is there something going on between Q and Quintana?"

"I'm not quite sure. I know he has a thing for her, and maybe she has a thing for him too. I sure would like to know what that note said, and why he received the only meal with fresh oysters," responds Indigo.

"Looks like baby bro may have found something that will keep him coming back to Dallas more and more, besides you that is," adds Keith.

ReGina Crawford

"Let's just pay the check, and finish our evening and let Q finish his without us speculating on its ending," states Kendrick as he starts to get up from the table.

Food From The Heart

Appetizer

Quentin enters the kitchen to find Quintana standing over one of the many stoves cooking up some sinfully looking dessert. She sees him from the corner of her eye, but doesn't miss a beat in what she's doing. Quentin merely waits patiently for her to finish; she's a joy to watch in the kitchen. Once the dessert is finished, she instructs a waiter which table to deliver it to, then takes Quentin's hand and leads him to her office. "What are you doing in my kitchen," she asks.

"Watching you, and you are a joy to watch," he answers. "I can tell that cooking is an art form to you, and I love your dedication. You didn't so as much as flinch when I came through those doors. If you keep impressing me like this, I won't think I'm worthy to take you out on a date."

"Oooh. You are smooth. Keep your butt in this office until the kitchen shuts down. My staff and I don't need the distraction of an observer, especially a drop dead sexy one." She laughs as he blushes from her compliment. Quentin occupies himself with the various cooking magazines and books on the table in front of him while he waits for the activity on the kitchen to settle down. He makes a note of a few recipes that he would like to taste while going through the books. However, the books don't hold his interest for long, so he watches Quintana through the windows in her office. He notices that she looks sluggish and tired, and wonders how long her day has been. As she wipes sweat from her forehead with her apron, Quentin decides to treat her to a night of pampering. He pulls out his cell phone and makes a few calls. Just as he completes all the arrangements, he hears Quintana telling one of her employees good night. He walks to the doorway of her office and notices that it is just her and the dishwasher left in the kitchen. He takes off his jacket and tie, rolls up his sleeves and heads in the direction of the dishwasher. "Just what do you think you are doing," Quintana asks him as he reaches Alejandro.

"I was hoping to relieve the dishwasher of his duties so that you and I might be alone," answers Quentin. Then in Spanish he asks Alejandro if he would like some paid time off, that he would finish the dishes. Alejandro and Quentin look at Quintana at the same time, and when she turns her back on them they take that as a yes. Quentin slips Alejandro a twenty for leaving early. Once the door closes behind the last employee, Quentin turns to Quintana. "Now are you going to show me how to work this thing or not?" She shows him how the dish washing equipment works and they finish the duties in companionable silence. Up close he can see just how long her day has been and that she is worn out. "How about I take you somewhere where you can get a nice body rub, sit in a Jacuzzi or a steaming sauna, and just relax?"

"That sounds wonderful, but we don't know each other that well."

"How else are we going to get to know each other if we don't spend some time together. I promise you it's your show, you will call all the shots. I am there merely to be your personal servant so that you don't have to do anything but take it easy. You look worn out, and I would just like to help you recover some of your energy and vitality. Can I do that?"

"It's my show? I'm calling all the shots?"

"Yes and yes."

"Okay. What do you have in mind?"

Food From The Heart

"All you need to do is follow me. I'm even willing to let you drive your own car, so you can leave any time you're ready. Is that fair enough?"

"Sounds fair to me." She follows him to the parking lot. When she reaches her car, he takes the keys from her hand, opens the door, and helps her inside before going to his own car. She follows him into the parking lot of the Grand Kempenski Hotel, "I'm, impressed," she states out loud. She parks her car beside his, and he is at her door before she can open it. Again he opens the door for her, helps her out, and leads her to the hotel. After stopping at the front desk for the key to the room, they take the elevator to the room he has reserved for them. Once inside the room, she asks, "How long have you been planning this?"

"Actually, I had to call in quite a few favors tonight to pull this off, but don't worry it's all legit. Now in the bedroom to the left you will find everything you need, so go change into the bathing suit, and I'll start the Jacuzzi." She does as instructed, and is amazed to find in the bedroom a bathing suit, a nightgown, robe, slippers, and a change of clothes. She changes into the bathing suit and returns to the sitting area. Quentin emerges from the bedroom on the right in a bathing suit of his own, if you could call the skimpy piece of material he was wearing a suit. "Wonderful, you're ready," he states as he enters the sitting area. He leads her to the Jacuzzi, helps her down the steps and settles her into one of the seats. The jet sprays of warm water caress her body and massage away the day's fatigue.

As the tension in her body fades away, she looks at Quentin sitting across from her and smiles. "This is just what I needed, and I would never have done this myself. Thank you."

"You are quite welcome. It is my pleasure to serve you, just tell me what you need or desire."

"Well I remember something about a body rub."

ReGina Crawford

"If that's what you want, that's what you will get." He reaches behind him for a bottle of scented body oil before scooting closer to her. He begins with her feet, then her legs and thighs. When he's ready to do her back, he holds out his hand to her, and she gladly places her hand in his. He pulls her towards him and turns her around before going to work on her neck, shoulders, and back. She feels like a limp rag doll by the time he's finished. "You look like you're ready to fall asleep. Let's get you to bed." He helps her out of the tub, wraps a towel around her, and leads her in the direction of her room. He stops at the door, kisses her hand, and says good night.

Food From The Heart

Late Night Snack

She stands there and watches him walk back in the direction of the Jacuzzi. He doesn't turn back in her direction once. "I'm all for chivalry, but he could have at least made it seem like it was hard for him to resist coming inside the room with me." She enters the room, showers, and puts on the nightgown, robe and slippers. Wide awake after her shower, she heads for the Jacuzzi where he finds Quentin with a drink in his hand and his eyes closed. "Do you plan on sleeping in there all night," she asks.

Having heard her enter the room, Quentin is not startled by her voice. He slowly opens his eyes, and what he sees leaves him speechless. She's beautiful with her hair loose and flowing around her face and shoulders. She didn't belt the robe, and at the angle at which he is looking at her the light shines right through the material of the gown and robe. He could see every wonderful curve of her body. "I haven't been as successful with my own body as I have been with yours, so I thought maybe a few more minutes in here and another drink ought to put me to sleep."

She walks over to him and takes the drink from his hand, shaking her head no when he starts to protest. She pulls his hand to let him know she wants him to get out of the pool. He does what she wants since he told her she was calling all the shots tonight. She takes him through the sitting room to his room and on to the connecting bathroom, and turns on the shower. She strips down before removing his trunks, and pulls him into the shower with her. Neither one has said a word, they just go with the flow. She lathers him up and rinses him off before turning off the water. She takes a towel and dries him off from head to toe, before wrapping the towel around his waist. She then dries herself off before leading him back to the bed where she lies him on his stomach, and prepares to give him a backrub while completely nude. After a few minutes, his muscles are still tense and tight. "Quentin, just let the tension flow right out of you, relax."

"Quintana," he whispers. She doesn't answer. "Quintana," he says again a little louder. Her only response is an 'Hmm'. "I know that you don't have on a stitch behind me, and it's driving me crazy. I don't think you should be doing this. I think you should go to your room and get some rest."

"You're thinking too much. Don't think, just feel."

"If I go with what I'm feeling, I'll be flipping you over on your back. I'm not trying to scare you sweetheart, but I think it only fair that I warn you how close to the edge I am. I want to make love to you, but that is not the reason I brought you here. I wanted to do something special just for you and only you."

"And I must say that you accomplished your goal. I feel wonderful, but I also wanted to touch you, to feel your skin beneath my palms, and if that makes you want to make love to me . . .," she pauses. "Well let's just say, I'm not going to stop you."

As the last word leaves her mouth, she finds herself flipped over on her back with Quentin on his elbows above her. "Are you sure you know what you're doing?" As she nods her head yes, he continues, "Right now I have the control needed to let you walk out of this room, but if I touch you, kiss you, it will be all over for me. I don't want you waking up tomorrow morning with regrets that you spent the night in my bed. Is that what you want, to spend the night in my bed?"

Food From The Heart

In answer to his question, she lifts her head and laves his left nipple with her tongue. He moans as a shudder courses through his body from the feel of her tongue on his chest. She laves the right one to confirm her answer. She looks up at his face, but his eyes are closed and his neck is arched back, so she can't get a clear view of his face and his emotions. A second later, he looks down at her, and what she sees in his eyes cause her to stop breathing momentarily. Never before has seen passion so hot in anyone's eyes before. "Don't fight it, you can't possibly win," she whispers.

He groans before capturing her mouth in a red hot kiss unleashing all the passion inside of him. She wraps her arms around his neck preparing to hold on tight for she knows this ride will be rough. Feeling her arms around his neck, he tears off his towel and presses himself against her belly. He needs contact with her flesh, but doesn't trust himself to enter her body right now. He knows he has got to cool some of his desire for her so that he doesn't hurt her when he comes inside of her.

She feels him pressing against her stomach, and believes she knows just what he needs. She reaches between them, and caresses him with her hand. His whole body jerks at the contact of his flesh with her hand. He rolls to the side to give her better access to him. She continues to stroke him with her hand until he feels his body tighten as he nears the ultimate pleasure. She increases the motion of her strokes, and he growls out at his release. She continues to stroke him until she is sure that all his desire for the moment is spent. She leans up and kisses him while he recovers.

"I can't believe you did that. I can't believe I let you do that. Why did you do that," he finally asks.

"Because I could see and feel how strongly you needed relief. So, I thought I would provide you with the relief you needed. Am I right?"

ReGina Crawford

"Yes, now I can love you like you deserved to be loved." He gives her another of his red hot kisses while he runs his hand over her breasts, stomach, and thighs. "I love the feel of your skin beneath my fingers. It's so smooth and warm, and I just want to touch you and taste you all over." He proceeds to do just that beginning at her jaw line, going down her neck to her breasts, stomach, waist, hips, then thighs. As he begins his assent back up her body, he finally looks at the apex of her thighs and the dark brown silky curls covering her womanhood. He gently runs his fingers through the curls, then parts them so that he can see the essence of her sexuality. He touches her there, she whimpers. He touches her again, and again she whimpers. He gently strokes her with his tongue and she purrs from deep in her throat. That was all the incentive he needed. He loves her completely with his mouth until she is yelling out his name over and over. He stays nestled between her thighs with his chin resting on top of her woman's mound until she has fully recovered. When she opens her eyes and looks down at him, he smiles. "Hello there. I was wondering when you were going to join me again."

"I must admit I was wondering how long it would be before I recovered. You don't do anything half measure, do you?"

"I must admit I have no liking for half measures or condensed versions of anything. I prefer to have the total experience to base my feelings on. Now I know when the night started I said this was your show and that you called all the shots, so I'm giving you one last chance to take refuge in your room." He shakes his head as she begins to speak. "Before you say anything let me say this. If you agree to stay, it becomes my show. I take over and love you as completely as I know how. There will be no calling 'Uncle' once I have begun, you'll have to stay with me for the duration of the experience. Not trying to be cocky or over confident, but this is bound to be an all night matinee. Are you ready for that?"

"If I'm not, I'm sure you won't let me fall too far behind."

Food From The Heart

He grins before lowering his head to taste her sweetness once again. She arches her hips violently at the feel of his hot mouth on her. She had no idea he would want dessert after the meal he just had. What has she just consented to? He takes his time savoring every movement of her hips, every cry from her lips, the taste of her femininity. Just when she reaches the highest level of sensitivity she's capable of achieving, he takes her over the edge. He doesn't touch her, but moves up beside her to watch her as she recovers. The kaleidoscope of expressions that pass across her face as she recovers lets him know he has given her the ultimate pleasure. When her body feels like her own again, she opens her eyes to look directly into his, and they both smile at each other. "Glad you came back to join me."

"So am I. I just have one question. Does the matinee include role reversal?"

"If you are so inclined, I think I can indulge you in that."

"Good. My turn," she states as she rolls him onto his back and treats his body to the same attention and dedication with which he treated hers. She climbs up on his chest to nibble on his ears which causes him to moan. She then licks her way across his body starting at his neck to his chest, and each of his nipples turn into hard little pebbles with the attention she gives them. So far he has maintained his control and his composure. She makes her way across his stomach to his hips, leaving hot little kisses in her wake. When she runs her tongue across his hip bone, he nearly jumps off the bed. She sits back and looks at him. The look on his face is one of surprise, letting her know that no one has ever done that to him before and that he didn't know that the spot was sensitive. He sees the gleam in her eyes and tries to prevent her from repeating the action. "I don't recall stopping you, but I do recall something about the total experience. Lay back and enjoy."

She runs her tongue slowly across his hip, his body tenses up as he is overwhelmed by the sensation. She decides to come back to that spot a little later, and proceeds to lick her way down the outside of his thigh. She can tell by his moans, and the clenching of his hands into fists that he has yet to receive a 'total experience'. Well isn't he in for a treat. When she reaches his knee, she nudges him to roll over onto his side and she licks her way up the back of his thigh to his bottom. She licks and kisses his behind until he's trembling. She rolls him flat on his stomach and learns just how sensitive his back and neck are, and so does he. She treats his other butt cheek and thigh to the same treatment the other side received before allowing him to turnover onto his back again. His breathing is ragged, he's biting his lip, and she loves every minute of it.

She finally settles herself between his legs, and he grips the edges of the bed for support. In an effort to help him through the experience, she takes him completely into her mouth. His hips arch off the bed and a low ragged moan escapes his lips. She then begins to play, placing little kisses and licks all over his throbbing member. She keeps this up until he can stand no more. "I'm . . . at my . . . limit . . . baby please . . . stop," he pleads. She takes him completely into her mouth and suckles until he finds his release. Smiling, she climbs up beside him while he recovers from her love making. "That's twice you've done that to me," he states several minutes later, "and now we are going to sleep."

"What happened to the total experience," she quips with a smile on her face.

"Oh you're going to get it, just not tonight. I think you've had enough for one night. Go to sleep."

Quintana snuggles closer to Quentin, and goes to sleep with a smile on her face. Quentin however isn't so lucky. He keeps feeling her hands and mouth all over his body, and he can't seem to get his body to settle down which has never happened to him before. He eventually falls asleep with Quintana wrapped tightly in his arms.

Food From The Heart

Breakfast

Quintana slowly awakens with a smile on her face from the dream she was having about being wrapped in Quentin's arms. Then it dawns on her that she is wrapped in someone's arms, and her eyes spring open. She looks up into Quentin's smiling face, and the look of surprise on her face lets him know that she thought it was all a dream. He starts to chuckle, and she frowns. He places a kiss in the middle of her forehead.

"Thought it was all a dream huh," he asks around his smile.

Quintana can't help but smile at him, "Yeah, I kinda did."

"Well then let me show you that it was not a dream," he states before giving her a slow mind drugging kiss. Once he feels her melt like butter in his arms, he breaks the kiss.

Once she regains her composure she states, "I never did get the total experience last night, so what are my chances of getting it this morning?"

"Are you sure you want to go there?"

"I got the feeling that I ventured into some unexplored territory last night. So it seems that you've never really had a total experience. You may have given them, but you haven't received any. And I'm about to change that. I don't believe in letting the man do all the work or having all the fun. So my question to you is, are you ready for that?"

"Someone once said, 'If I'm not, I'm sure you won't let me fall too far behind', and I think that fits perfectly." They laugh as they hug and kiss. As the kiss intensifies, the laughter dies down. Quentin rolls Quintana onto her back and fits himself between her legs. He slowly seeks entrance into her center, she's wet but she's tight and he finds this to be a turn on beyond his wildest imagination. He withdraws, makes another attempt, doesn't get much further, and withdraws again. Several attempts later he is finally half way inside her. "Sweetheart, you are so tight. I'm trying to go slow so I don't hurt you, but it's driving me crazy. I'm going to put your legs over my shoulders." He does just that, but needs her legs spread wider and lets them drop down to rest on his biceps. A few attempts later, he is buried to the hilt inside her. She is griping him like a new glove. He remains still letting her adjust to him. "If you only knew how you feel to me," he unwittingly says out loud.

"If it feels anything like you feel to me, then we both must be in heaven," she replies as her inner muscles squeeze around him.

"Oh God," he cries and begins moving inside her. He withdraws almost completely, places her feet flat on his chest, then plunges deep. "Quintana," he chants as he repeats the motion until she is yelling out his name in her release. He lets her legs slide down his chest until they are resting on each side of him. Then he rolls onto his back bringing her with him until she's settled on top of him. He gives her a couple of minutes to recover before he begins to move her hips with his hands, but it isn't long before she takes over.

She starts out slow and easy, but as he bucks against her rhythm, she picks up the tempo of her movements. It's not long before she's chanting his name during her climax. Once she's breathing steady enough to talk, she says, "I'm not going to survive another one of those. My body is already a mass of raw sensations."

Food From The Heart

"I'm afraid this interlude is not yet over. You've only reached your peak twice, and I've yet to have my breakfast. I think you can stand a few more with at least two of them in my mouth."

She closes her eyes at the thought of him putting his mouth on her body. "If I give you what you want, are you going to give me what I want?"

"And just what is it that you want?"

"I want breakfast too. The question is, are you going to give it to me?"

"Sweetheart I would love to give it to you, however, the next time I come I want it to be with me inside you. And since you stole two from me last night, I only have one more left to give." She begins pouting but he knows how to put a smile on her face, and he reaches between their bodies and slowly caresses her. "You're so wet. So hot," he whispers in her ear as he continues to stroke her while laying her flat on her back. As she begins to move her hips to the rhythm of his fingers, he leans over and kisses the moans from her lips. She reaches another orgasm in no time at all. "And you thought you couldn't survive another one," he states as her breathing returns to normal. "Now it's time for my breakfast," he states as he slowly slides down her body placing hot little kisses on her breasts and stomach on the way down.

He doesn't waste any time getting what he wants. He simply grips her hips while plunging his tongue deep inside her sweet center. After circling her with his tongue a few times, he takes her lodestone into his mouth to suckle. It doesn't take her long to come apart to the rhythm of his mouth; however, he doesn't stop tasting her. The second orgasm arrives shortly after the first. He slides up her body and turns her on her side to face him while she recovers.

Unable to speak, she simply smiles while shaking her head at him. He then places her leg over his hip as he slowly enters her once again. His entrance is unhindered this time, and he revels in the moist hot feel of her. He loves her slowly and completely until they reach their peak together. His release is so powerful, he is still trembling several minutes later. Kissing him on the lips, Quintana states, "That's what I like to see, a man whose not so macho that he's unwilling to let his lady see the effect she has on him. Sweetheart I could get use to this in no time at all. A man who knows how to satisfy and is willing to let the lady satisfy him as well is hard to find."

"I plan to see that you do get use to it. I have no intention of going anywhere anytime soon." He states as he kisses her love swollen lips.

"I don't remember seeing you around before this week. I thought you were only in town for the wedding, although you are a little early."

"I'm more than a little early, the wedding isn't for another three months. Right now I am on an assignment from work, but I will be moving here permanently a few weeks before the wedding. It's my wedding gift to her so don't tell her. She thinks that I will be on vacation after my assignment so I can be here for the wedding, but I'll actually be running my office."

"What exactly is it that you do anyway?"

"What I'm about to tell you doesn't leave this room, my front as a real estate developer must stay intact. I am an FBI agent, exactly." She simple stares at him with a stunned look on her face. "What? Why are you staring at me? Did I suddenly grow two heads or something?"

She snaps out of her trance to answer, "You just don't strike me as the FBI type. I always pictured those guys as having no sense of humor or style."

Food From The Heart

"That's why I'm so effective, I don't look like the average agent. People don't become suspicious of me the moment they see me, and I get them to relax and tell me things they wouldn't tell just anyone. That's why I got this plum assignment. I won't have to do much detective work. They'll be coming to me in droves."

"It's not going to be dangerous, is it?"

"It won't be anything I can't handle."

"That's what Kyle thought before too, and look what happened to him. I don't want to get tangled up with someone who is on the firing line day and night. I don't want to spend my nights in front of the TV news holding my breath and hoping that I don't hear your name being mentioned in a shootout."

He wraps his arms around her and pulls her close. "I don't do those kind of assignments. I merely set the people up with the right people to take them down. Otherwise I wouldn't be able to stay in one place too long. Everyone would get to know me as an agent. No one ever sees me as an agent except for the people in the agency. Now it's getting late, and I know you have a restaurant to open."

ReGina Crawford

Check In

As Quintana goes to the other room to shower and dress, Quentin lays there thinking. What has come over him? He's told this woman he barely knows more than his own sister. He knows why he hasn't told any of this to Indigo, she would worry herself sick and he didn't want that just before her wedding. But why has he told Quintana? It can't be the sex, he's had good sex before, granted not as good as this, but it's never made him tell all before. Is this the woman he's been waiting for? His mate for life? Was he ready for that? He loves the challenges of his career, and isn't ready to give it up. But could he have a family and his career at the same time? Time would tell. He finally gets up to get dressed himself.

They meet in the sitting room and he hands her a business card with all his numbers on it, and tells her to call him anytime she wants to hear his voice. They kiss before leaving the room. Once in their respective cars, they wave good-bye as they drive off in different directions.

When Quentin arrives back at Indigo's, Kyle, Indigo, Keith, and Jade are all sitting in the living room waiting for his arrival. "Hello everyone," he states as he attempts to walk past them to the bedroom.

"My brother, my brother. I know you don't think we just happen to be sitting here shooting the breeze as you finally make your way through the door." At his *should-I-know-where–this-conversation-*

Food From The Heart

is-going look, Kyle continues, "Have a seat. We are having a little family pow-wow."

Quentin reluctantly sits down in the only available spot, the recliner which happens to be positioned right between the two couples. "And might I ask why a 'family pow-wow' is necessary, especially on a Saturday?"

"Well we were all kind of worried when you didn't come home last night or earlier this morning. No one knew where you were at, and we want to make sure that this doesn't happen again."

"Excuse me? Last time I looked I was a grown man. Indigo, you are only a year older than I am, so don't try to play 'Mommy' with me. Jade same goes for you too. As for you other two, don't let these women railroad you into believing I'm some wayward child who needs guidance. I assure you I don't. I have been taking care of myself for quite some time now, and if I wasn't responsible the company wouldn't be giving me my own office down here. Now, as far as I'm concerned, the 'pow-wow' is over."

Stunned, they all look at each other as Quentin gets up and walks back to the bedroom. "He has a real job," asks a Jade.

"He's moving here," states a dazed Indigo.

The men look at each other then at the women before stating, "It appears you two don't know as much about Quentin as you thought."

The men then head for the bedroom, leaving the ladies in their confusion in the living room. They don't knock, they just enter the room. "Before you go ballistic, hear us out," states Kyle as he closes the door behind him and Keith. "Indigo nor Jade thought that you had a serious job or that you were responsible since you've never told them who you work for or what you do. The only way we are going to be able to keep them out of your business is to know what that business is. Beside we're cops, we're bound to find out one way or another."

"Okay fellas, I see what this is leading up to, so let me enlighten you before you get any more bright ideas." Quentin picks up his wallet from the top of the dresser and shows them his FBI ID and badge. "I see I have left you two stunned now as well. I don't want Indigo and Jade to know about this now or ever. I am never seen on the streets as an agent, so I won't be the target of some misguided criminal. So there is nothing for them to be concerned about, but I know if they knew they would be concerned about me anyway just like they are about the two of you."

"I'll be damned. The boy has more clout that we do, and he's moving to our city."

"Well if that don't beat all, but it will be nice having someone around who has some inside information on criminal activity in this town," adds Keith.

"Now wait a minute. I don't recall saying anything about sharing information with the two of you. Don't start looking at me like that." At their joined 'Like what', Quentin responds, "Like if you don't get what you want, you'll resort to blackmail. Come on fellas, you don't want your ladies worrying about me like they do you, do you?"

"I suppose we can keep quiet if you just drop us some hints every now and then about the underground activities taking place in the city," states Kyle.

"I'll see what I can do. Now can I get some rest?"

"Long night," quips Kyle.

"Something like that," replies Quentin with a grin.

Food From The Heart

"Care to share any of it with us," asks Keith.

"No," replies Quentin as he turns his back on them and finishes removing his clothing. They take the hint and head out the room. "Just thinking about last night turns me on, so I know reliving it through words would be hell." He then lies across the bed still grinning from the memories he allows himself to think about.

Kyle and Keith join Indigo and Jade in the kitchen, and let them know that they have nothing to worry about. Quentin is a good kid, and has his life on the right track and he'll tell them about his job when he wakes up from his nap. The ladies thank the men by placing kisses on their cheeks. They then head outdoors for some fun in the sun.

Quentin wakes up several hours later to discover himself alone in the house. Taking note of the time, he gets dressed and heads over to look at the condo he's just purchased. It's got high ceilings and practically no walls. It will almost resemble his loft in New York when he's done with the remodeling. He doesn't like to feel like he's boxed in, and having no walls gives him the freedom he needs. He can picture where everything will go, and then wonders if Quintana will like it. "Where the hell did that come from," he asks himself out loud. "A woman at my place, unheard of," he continues to himself. Then again this woman has affected him like no other woman he's met before, but he still needs to take it one day at a time. He makes another round of the place, taking mental notes on the placement of his belongs.

Dinner Break

When he arrives back at Indigo's there is a bouquet of balloons on the kitchen counter with a card that has his name written across the front. He opens the card which reads:

> *A token of my appreciation for the care*
> *and consideration I received at your hands.*
> *Thinking of you*
> *Quintana*

Quentin smiles, then looks at the balloons which are shaped like budding roses. Just as he places the card back in its envelope, in walks Indigo. "Well it seems someone has made an impression," she states while looking pointedly at the balloons.

"So it seems," quips Quentin. "Now about my moving here." He holds up a hand to keep her from speaking, "I was going to save this as a wedding present for you, but I think I'll tell you now. My company is setting up an office here, and I am going to run the office. Since I might have to do some entertaining and you will be a newlywed, I bought a condo outside downtown. It almost looks like my loft in New York so I think I'll be comfortable there. I know you thought the real estate thing was just a phase, but I'm good at it and obviously the company thinks I'm ready for more responsibility. I don't want you worrying about me, I'm a big boy and can take care of myself. Okay?"

Food From The Heart

"Okay. But you'll always be my baby brother," she smiles as she punches him in the arm.

"Ouch," he whines trying to pretend that her punch really hurt. She laughs as she walks away. "In our younger days, that would at least get me a hug and some ice cream." She laughs even harder as she continues to walk away. "Well so much for being her baby brother." He gets himself a soda and heads for the back porch off Indigo's bedroom where he finds Kyle stretched out on a lawn chaise with Indigo straddling him and giving him a rub down. "Must be nice man, having someone to take care of your aching muscles."

"It's wonderful," mumbles Kyle.

"Didn't I take care of yours last night," asks Quintana as she enters the side gate.

Stunned, Quentin blushes first before saying in a low voice, "Yes, yes you did." She walks up and kisses him on the lips. "How did you know we were back here," he asks at the end of the kiss.

"One of Indigo's neighbors told me as I was about to get back in my car when no one answered the door."

"Aren't you supposed to be at work," Quentin asks as an afterthought.

"It's like this, I've got the boss wrapped around my little finger and she lets me take off whenever I want." Quentin starts laughing. "What? You don't think I'm capable of wrapping someone around my finger?"

"No I believe you are plenty capable," he responds. Then for her ears only, he says, "You showed me just how capable last night." Then in his normal voice, he adds, "By the way thanks for the roses."

ReGina Crawford

"You're quite welcome. It was my pleasure."

"Mine too. Mine too," responds Quentin forgetting that he and Quintana were not alone.

"Do you two need some privacy? Not that we mind the show. I just figured I would remind you that you are not alone," states Indigo.

Quentin blushes again as he takes Quintana's hand and leads her into the house. Once inside his room, he pulls her into his arms, "Now for a proper thank you," he states before giving her a kiss that has her going up in flames.

Once she's able to breathe again, Quintana quips, "If that's how you say thank you, I'm going to have to send you a gift every day."

"Sweetheart you don't have to send me gifts for me to say thank you. Just be you and hang in there with me, and I'll say thank you everyday we're together."

"I believe I can handle that," she states as she leans up to kiss him once again. That kiss leads to another and another, and before she knows it she's half dressed. Quentin loves her breasts with his hot wet mouth, and her knees are getting weak. Quentin backs her up against the bed before lying her down and coming down over her. He never breaks contact with her breasts. Caught up in the raging inferno her body has become, she is not aware of the rest of her clothing being removed but she does become aware when he glides his tongue across the center of her. She's already wet, and he can't believe that his kisses have that effect on her. He licks her like a melting ice cream cone on a hot July day. Unable to help herself, Quintana screams "Quentin. Oh God," as she reaches her peak.

Kyle and Indigo are just coming in from the outside when they hear Quintana scream. They rush in the room to find Quentin nestled between Quintana's legs, and his face buried between her thighs.

Food From The Heart

Indigo covers her face with her hands as Kyle ushers her back out the door.

"And he had the nerve to talk about your dedication. He didn't flinch either because someone walked in the room," states Indigo once she recovers from her shock.

"What are you talking about," asks Kyle.

"Remember when he walked in on us the night he arrived?" At his nod, she continues, "Well the next day Quentin was teasing me about how you didn't so much as flinch when he walked in the room. He called you a glutton."

"Oh really. Well, I see I'll just have to pay him back for that little remark. Although he was telling the truth, I am a glutton when it comes to you," he states huskily as he corners her against the wall to run his tongue over her neck and shoulders.

Quentin sits next to Quintana on the bed waiting for her to recover. Once she does, he tells her of their visitors, and to be ready for some good natured teasing since he has done the same thing to them. Quintana is truly embarrassed, but Quentin assures her that there is nothing to be embarrassed about. Not with his sister and Kyle. She doesn't look convinced, so to take her mind off of it he begins to kiss her all over her body. She reaches her peak to the rhythm of his mouth once again. Quentin removes his clothing while she recovers from her orgasm. When she opens her eyes and sees his jutting manhood, she reaches out to caress him. He tightens up at her touch, while his throbbing shaft jerks violently after the caress. She continues to run her hand up and down and around the length of him until he is hissing his breath through his teeth. Then she takes him into her hot moist mouth, and loves him until he can't take any more. He moves them to the center of the bed, and spreads her legs over his shoulders and enters her in one swift thrust. They both growl yes at the time of entry. The ride is long and rough, but they both love every minute of it.

Quentin recovers first, and looks into her eyes. "Now that I have temporarily satisfied my hunger for you, I have to ask why you came by? Not that I mind, not at all. You have certainly made my evening, but I assume you had a reason for coming by."

After flicking her tongue across his nipple, she answers, "Yes, I did have a reason for coming by today, and you have already taken care of it." At the incredulous look on his face, she continues, "You did such a wonderful job on me last night, I had to see if it was real or just a dream. And believe me you have adequately shown me that it is real. I just might become addicted to you."

"That's good to know since I think I'm already addicted to you," he states before kissing her, imitating the thrusting of his body with his tongue. Quintana is instantly aroused, and they make love once again. "Oh sweetheart," begins Quentin while trying to regulate his breathing, "the things you make me feel, I've never felt before."

"What do you mean," asks Quintana while trying to regulate her own breathing.

"Never has an orgasm overwhelmed me like it does with you, and never has the fourth had the same impact as the first," he replies.

"Good, because I plan to keep you coming back for more."

"I'd say your plan is working. Now let's get you showered and dressed. I'm sure your boss expects you to show up for work sometime tonight."

"You're right. What time is it?

Quentin looks at his watch on the nightstand. It's almost nine o'clock. "It's quarter to nine," he half whispers expecting her to be upset that it's so late.

Food From The Heart

"You're kidding right," she asks rather calmly. He shakes his head no, and she just stares at him. "I've been here for over three hours? You're right, I need to get showered and dressed." He leads her to the bathroom and they shower together. They go back to the room to dress, and he escorts her to the front door. He closes the door after she drives off letting out a sigh of relief that Kyle and Indigo seem to have left the house.

However, he's in for a surprise when he turns around and sees them standing in the doorway to the kitchen. "Okay, let's have it. I know you two are dying to let it out."

"What could you possibly be talking about," asks Indigo unable to stop herself from laughing.

"You know exactly what I'm talking about. All the teasing I gave to you is about to come back to me ten-fold, isn't it?"

"Why ever would I do something like that?"

"Because I enjoyed my teasing of you so much. I know you can't wait to rub my face in this."

"Oh I think your face has been deep in it enough today," quips Indigo before falling into a fit of laughter.

"Touché Sis. I set myself up for that one."

"You certainly did my brother," chimes in Kyle. "Now I believe I heard something about dedication and gluttony, didn't I?"

"Yes sweetheart, you did," responds Indigo having recovered from her laughter.

"Now you were with the lady all night and a few hours this morning, then again this evening. If that's not dedication and gluttony, I don't know what is," states Kyle.

"I admit it, okay? I have fallen into the same trap as you have. Apparently Indigo and Quintana have seized control of us man, and we are powerless to fight it. Though I must admit, I'm loving every minute of it and wouldn't want to fight it."

"I hear you. I feel the same way."

"How can you take his side in this," asks Indigo trying to pretend outrage.

"What can I say? I love the way you occupy my heart, body, and soul. And I can relate to how the man feels. When a man finds a woman who makes him feel the way you make me feel, he can't walk away from her no matter how hard he tries."

"Since you put it that way, okay. Teasing is over, for now."

"Thanks Sis."

"You're welcome Bro."

Food From The Heart

Revelations

Quentin changes clothes to go for a late night run before going to bed. While he is out running, he sees what appears to be some kind of underground deal going down. Not wanting to appear interested in what was going on, he continues running at the same pace until he rounds a corner. Then he starts doing double time to make it back to the scene of the meeting. He creeps down the alley in between two buildings, then crouches down to listen to what's being said.

"I don't want anybody killed, I just want them taught a lesson," states a gentleman in a long leather trench coat and alligator skin boots.

"I understand Mr. Red," states the gentleman directly across from him in snake skin boots, "They'll get the message loud and clear sir."

'Red' hands the other gentle man a large manila envelope, they shake hands and then move off to their respective cars. Quentin is wondering who the gentlemen are, and who is going to be taught a lesson. He holds his place several minutes after the two cars leave the scene just to be sure that he is not seen. It was a good thing that he did, because just as he was thinking about standing a third car pulled away from the curb with its lights off. "Now who the hell was that, and who were they watching," Quentin asks himself.

He finally stands and scans the street again, but the rest of the cars appear to be unoccupied and the street is clear. However, just to be safe, he leaves the way he came. Once he arrives at Indigo's, Quentin calls his superiors and tells them of the events he witnessed. They tell him to keep his ears and eyes open about anyone who appears to have been threatened in any way. He has a list of key underground players in the city, and what connections they have to each other. As far as he knows though, no one on the list had a beef with anyone else on the list, so who are the men he saw tonight. Quentin prepares himself mentally for a thorough investigation while he showers. After meditating for a half hour, Quentin crawls into bed totally relaxed and instantly falls asleep.

The next morning he takes a run down to the local newsstand to check out the morning headlines. From the looks of it, nothing happened last night. After jogging back home, he showers and dresses as a real estate broker scouting for new properties. As he drives through certain neighborhoods, he takes note of the players he's already familiar with, and any new faces he sees in the crowd. He also looks to see if any of them appear nervous or apprehensive. He notices nothing out of the ordinary. If only he had a time frame when he knew something was going to happen.

Unable to pick up on anything in the hood, Quentin heads over to his new offices. It isn't until he's out of the hood that he picks up the tail behind him. 'Let's see who is interested in me, and what they have in mind,' he thinks to himself. He leads the tail through a maze of streets before pulling up to his new offices. 'They need to know where to find me when the time comes to make some contacts with the underground,' is his thought as he gets out of the car and heads for the front appearing to be oblivious to the tail. Just as reaches the door and is about to insert the key in the lock, a female hand covers the key hole. He slowly follows the hand up the arm across bare shoulders, up the neck to a gorgeous face. He whistles unable to help himself. "I'm not officially open yet, but for you I'll make an exception." She doesn't say a word, just merely arches a perfectly shaped eyebrow.

Food From The Heart

He moves her hand and opens the door before turning and saying, "Come on in." He opens the blinds slightly to let in some light, before pulling his chair around to the front of his desk since it's the only chair in the place. Only his things from New York have arrived already, the rest of the furniture should arrive in three to four days. "Have a seat," he states as he moves the chair next to her before having a seat on the corner of his desk. "I'm Quentin McNair, and you are," he asks after she takes a seat in the chair.

"My name is Sylvia Williams."

"Well Ms Williams, what brings you to my doorstep since I'm neither open nor advertising?"

"I followed you from the last vacant lot you were looking at, didn't you see my Mercedes behind you?"

"No, I'm afraid my mind was preoccupied with the buildings and land I saw today," he responds while thinking to himself why she would want him to know that she was following him. "Then I went sightseeing through the city to get a feel for the type of architecture used here. That must have been a really wild drive for you if you followed me from South Dallas. Why did you follow me?"

"Obviously, I thought you were someone or something you're not."

"Excuse me? Could you clarify that for me?"

"I thought that you were one of those alphabet boys," she responds, "or at least a real player looking for some action." At his raised eyebrow, she answers what she believes to be his question, "Alphabet boys, you know FBI, CIA, DEA, ATF, but since you don't notice when people are following you I guess you're none of the above. Although for a while during your sightseeing, I thought you were trying to lose me."

"Like I said, I didn't even know you were behind me, and I know I glanced in my rear view mirror quite a few times. I think I would have noticed you if you were behind me," he states out loud while thinking *'Why would I want to lose my first contact to the underground'*. "But why would you think I was one of the 'Alphabet Boys' as you call them?"

Ignoring his question, she responds, "Well I wasn't directly behind you, but that's not the point of my visit. Just exactly who are you Mr. McNair and what are you doing in my city?"

"I am merely a real estate broker whose company is expanding to this area, and since I have been broker of the year for the last two years I got first shot at this office. I can turn abandoned buildings and vacant lots into big money projects in no time at all. My boss says I have a great knack for seeing the potential in various locations. I told him it's because I get a vibe from the people of the city, and can feel what they want or need." Seeing that she is not impressed by what he has told her by the scowl on her face, Quentin states, "I get the feeling that you don't like me Ms Williams. Have I done something to offend you?"

"No, but keep in mind that I'll be watching you," she states just before she gets up and leaves.

When the door closes behind her, he states out loud, "I'll be watching you too." He reaches inside his pocket to turn off the tape recorder that he had running, and hopes that the surveillance camera got a good shot of her and her car. He locks the front door before going into the hidden back room to check the recording. "Great, I got a full facial view of you Ms Williams and your plate number," he states out loud. He removes the DVD and replaces it with a new blank one before leaving the room to send the audio and video off for identifying purposes.

Food From The Heart

Dessert

Once his task is complete, Quentin heads over to Quintana's restaurant for lunch, and hopefully a few minutes alone in her office. The crowd is light at eleven forty-five, so Quentin is able to be seated with no problem. He picks up his menu to make a selection, but before he reads through it, the menu is removed from his hands. He looks up into Quintana's eyes and immediately smiles as he leans back in his chair and folds his arms across his chest. "What are you doing here," asks Quintana through a smile.

"I'm trying to have lunch if I could get my menu back. A man has to eat you know, especially when he has a woman who drains him every chance she gets." A blush creeps up her cheeks at his words. "Oh, a little shy today, are we? You didn't appear to be too shy last night."

"Hush. Someone might hear you. Here take the menu, maybe with food in your mouth you'll keep your dirty thoughts to yourself."

"I'd rather have you in my mouth, but I'll settle for some of your cooking," he quips over his smile before laughing as her cheeks get redder. She walks away shaking her head, and he continues laughing as he looks over the menu once again. He enjoys his lunch while making notes about his earlier drive through the hood, and his visitor. Just as he is about to get up from the table, Quintana emerges from the kitchen. She doesn't say a word, merely takes his hand, and leads him back to her office. Once inside, she closes the door and all the blinds. "What is this all about," he asks when she turns to face him.

"Dessert," she replies as she walks into his arms and sucks his bottom lip into her mouth. He parts his lips and she eases her tongue into his mouth. He can't believe how weak her kisses make him feel, and she can't believe he's letting her do what she wants. She leaves his mouth to place a trail of kisses across his cheek to his ear and then on to his neck. "Hmm. You smell good," she states in between kisses.

Unable to take anymore, Quentin picks her up and carries her to the sofa and lies her down on it. He gets down on his knees beside the sofa and begins unbuttoning her blouse as he consumes her senses with his red hot kisses. Once he has the blouse completely open and her bra unfastened, he kisses a trail of fire to her breasts before applying the suction she adores. She arches her back giving him better access to her. Once he's satisfied that her breasts have been sufficiently loved, he kisses a trail down her stomach to the waist band of her pants. He pulls them off her hips with her help while inhaling her scent. He wastes no time burying his tongue deep inside her sweet heat since she did invite him into her office for dessert. Her moans and whimpers cause him to stop, "You're going to have to be quiet while I finish my dessert. I'd hate to be interrupted while enjoying a dish as tasty as this one." She grabs a pillow off the couch to yell into as he brings her to an explosive climax.

Her orgasm makes her want all of him, and she removes his jacket, tie and shirt caressing each bared inch of skin with her lips and tongue. Next thing Quentin knows, he's on the couch and she's on her knees unbuckling his belt. However, the sound of a metal platter hitting the floor in the kitchen snaps him back to reality. Quentin grabs her hands in his, and holds them until he can get his breathing and his pulse back under control. Once he has managed that, he smiles while shaking his head at her. "We are not going to do this

Food From The Heart

here in your office. What if someone walks in here? And don't say lock the door because we both know that there'll be enough noise coming from this room that everyone outside the room will know what was happening inside the room."

"You're right but I just couldn't help myself. Seeing you out there at that table just set me on fire. What have you done to me?"

"What have I done to you? What have you done to me? Whenever I'm around you I just can't seem to keep my hands or my mouth to myself. The sight of you, the smell of your perfume, the sexiness of your voice causes my blood to boil, and I can't think straight. Look what almost happened in here. It took every ounce of will power I have in me to pull away from you."

"I know sweetheart. Maybe we won't react so strongly to each other over time," she states while getting dressed. Then adds slightly under her breath, "Although I doubt that will happen."

"I heard that, and I must admit I agree with you. I've never reacted this strongly to anyone before. This is all new to me, and I'm not sure how to handle it."

"It's all new to me too," she responds. "What are we going to do," she asks as she gets dressed.

"I don't know, but I'm sure that we'll think of something."

"Why don't you stop by my place later tonight, so that we can discuss this further? Maybe we'll have thought of a solution by then."

"What time do you want me to stop by?"

"Around eleven thirty," she responds.

"I can make that. I'll see you then. Now walk me out so that everyone will know you're not still recovering from my love making," he quips as he stands.

"One look at your crotch, and they will know that nothing happened in here." They both burst into laughter, and Quentin buttons his jacket before opening the door.

Food From The Heart

Chance Meeting

Just as they exit the kitchen, Ms Sylvia Williams is being seated at the exact table Quentin occupied earlier. "Hi Sylvia," states Quintana as they reach the table. Quentin is chocked into silence that Quintana knows this woman.

"Hi Quintana, Mr. McNair," replies Sylvia maintaining her surprise that they both know Quintana.

However, Quintana is not as successful as Quentin and Sylvia at hiding her surprise that they have met. "You two have met," she asks looking back and forth between the two of them.

"We met this morning at my as yet unopened real estate office," volunteers Quentin.

"I saw him driving through the neighborhood, and decided to follow him to see where he would end up. Imagine my surprise when he stopped in front of what appeared to be an abandoned office building," adds Sylvia looking a little displeased at finding the two of them together.

"Oh. Well just so there's no misunderstanding, I saw him first," states Quintana while smiling at Sylvia.

"As much as I'm enjoying this conversation, I need to get going," Quentin states to the ladies. Then to Quintana, "I'll see you after work." He smiles revealing his dimple before turning and walking out of the restaurant.   As he gets inside his car he wonders to himself, "Is it just coincidence that you showed up at the restaurant today, or were you still following me? And how in the hell do you know Quintana? How is it that she doesn't know who you are? Well I plan to get to the bottom of this, and soon."

"Just how do you know this McNair person," asks Sylvia after Quentin walks through the door to the outside.

"He's the brother of the bride whose wedding I'm catering in a few months," answers Quintana. "Why?"

"Nothing that I can put my finger on. There just seems to be more than meets the eye with him. He claims to be a real estate broker and nothing more, but I just feel like he's hiding something."

"Why do you feel like he's hiding something?"

"Like I said I can't put my finger on it, but I will figure it out. Trust me on this one."

Quintana walks away, leaving Sylvia to her thoughts, hoping she doesn't find out who Quentin is if he doesn't want her to know. Then she wonders if Quentin can find out who she is, and if he even cares who she is. That's a stupid question, she thinks. If she followed him around town, he probably already put the wheels in motion to find out who she is, and if she can be of any use to him. Quintana wonders if she will be caught in between them since one is her friend and the other is her lover.

By the time Quentin makes it back to Indigo's there's a message waiting on him from headquarters. He calls in to see if they have any information on Ms. Williams. The phone is answered on the second ring. "Hey Brad, got your messages," states Quentin. After listening to Brad's reply greeting, Quentin asks, "Anything on Ms Williams?"

Food From The Heart

"Yes, and you're not going to believe what I'm about to tell you. I just want you to know I had to pull a lot of strings to get this information."

"Just spit it out," returns Quentin impatiently.

"She's an ex-undercover military operative. Apparently a few years ago a military unit was taken down by some Columbian drug lord, and her fiancée, brother, and a cousin were all a part of the unit. She has made it her mission in life to bring to justice all who were involved. She does not tolerate interference from anyone including the CIA and FBI, so be very careful around her my friend. We will do everything possible on this end to make sure your cover isn't blown, because if she finds out who you are she will put it on the local news so that no one will deal with you. She doesn't want anyone taking these guys down, she wants to be the one to do it and will get rid of anyone that she thinks is a threat to her mission. She's become somewhat of a renegade, and is somehow funding her own operation since her government funds were cut off ten months ago."

"Well I certainly wasn't expecting that bit of news, but it certainly makes things a little more interesting."

"Be careful man. I've talked with a couple of agents who have crossed paths with her before, and they say she's vicious and determined that no one else takes these guys down."

"Believe me, I plan to keep both eyes on her. She let me see her claws this morning though she didn't use them. I think she just wanted me to know that they were there. If there's any other information about her out there I want it. Friends, family, enemies, favorite restaurants, her gym, etc. I want it all since that is the only way I can keep from crossing her path accidentally. I especially want to know what her relationship is with Quintana Richardson."

"Sure thing man. I'll get right on it. Talk to you later."

ReGina Crawford

They hang up the phone and Quentin decides he needs to clear his head, so he puts on his gear and heads for Indigo's gym. After a two hour workout, he heads back to Indigo's to shower and change before heading over to his condo. There is still a lot of work to be done before he can move in. He wants to get the upper-landing built before he begins painting. After working non-stop since his arrival five hours before, Quentin decides to take a break. He turns to look out the window and notices how dark it is outside, and looks around for his watch. It's a quarter after ten, "Damn, I'm going to have to rush if I'm going to make it to Quintana's by eleven-thirty." He grabs the rest of his stuff, and heads home for another shower. When he arrives at the house he notices that Indigo's car is not there, "Good. I won't have to explain where I'm going or why I'm in a rush to get there."

Food From The Heart

Joy and Pain

He arrives at Quintana's at eleven-thirty on the dot, and she is just pulling up herself. "Hello," she says huskily as she gets out of the car.

"Hello yourself," he returns the greeting as they walk to the front door. Once inside, he pulls her into his arms for a kiss. She doesn't even try to stop him in any way, and before she knows it she's as bare as the day she was born. "Where's the bedroom," he asks as he picks her up in his arms.

"Upstairs, but let's make it the bathroom. I need a shower," she replies.

"The bathroom it is then," he responds as he carries her up the stairs.

Once inside the bathroom, he undresses as she gets the shower started and steps inside. He joins her moments later, and they raise the temperature in the shower as they caress each other as they wash each other's bodies. Soon cleansing each other is the farthest thing from their minds as Quentin begins using his lips and tongue to caress her body. Before she knows it, Quintana is climaxing in the shower to the rhythm of his mouth. While she is still recovering from her orgasm, Quentin turns off the shower and carries her to her bedroom after wrapping her in a towel. He takes his time drying off her warm aroused body alternately using the towel and his mouth. By the time he's done. Quintana is breathing hard and well on her way to another orgasm. Quentin lays her across her bed, and makes short work of bring her to a climax once again with his mouth. As she recovers once again, he dries his body with a towel while smiling down at the woman still experiencing aftershocks from his loving.

Just as he is about to join her on the bed, Quintana sits up on the side of the bed and takes his throbbing member in her hand to slowly caress. A ragged moan escapes from his lips at her touch, and this encourages her to flick the tip of her tongue across the tip of him. He grabs her hands and takes a step back, "Sweetheart, you know I wouldn't deny you anything, but I have to stop you this time. I just can't take any more. I want to be inside you now."

Smiling, she nods her head yes in acquiescence while saying, "I'm going to let you pass this time, but you definitely owe me and more than one."

He smiles while laying her back across the bed, and sliding in between her legs. Even though they made love yesterday, she is tight again and it isn't until his fourth attempt that he manages full penetration. The ride is rough but she doesn't mind, and they explode together.

Sometime later, after they are both breathing normally again, Quentin asks Quintana the question that has been running around inside his head for most of the day. "How do you know Sylvia Williams?"

Quintana leans up on one elbow to look at him before asking, "Where did that come from? Please don't tell me you've been lying here in my bed thinking about another woman."

Quentin, who had been absentmindedly rubbing her back, is slightly startled by her reaction. He sits up in bed and turns them so they are facing each other. "First, after what we have shared the last few days, how could you think that I would want to be with another

Food From The Heart

woman that way," he asks. However, before she could answer the question he continues, "Second, if you're the jealous suspicious type, you need to tell me now. Last but not least, I am an FBI agent. When someone, male or female, makes it a point to follow me around town for half an hour, I want to know who they are and which side they are on - mine or the other guys. Unfortunately my business happens to intrude at inopportune moments, of which this happens to be one, but you two seemed to know each other quite well and I was wondering what you could tell me about her. That is all there is to it." He sits there staring into her eyes, barely containing the disappointment he feels at her statement.

Quintana sits there staring back at him trying to digest all the words she just received from him, and holding her breath waiting to see what his next move will be. When she doesn't say anything right away, Quentin makes a move to get out of bed. Quintana lets loose the breath she was holding while she reaches out to touch his arm. "Don't go," she whispers. He turns back in her direction, and sees tears falling from her eyes. He's confused and it shows on his face. She closes her eyes and takes a deep breath, "Where do I begin," she states while trying to regain her composure. "Sylvia's fiancé was my brother. You don't seem to be surprised so I gather you know who she is." At his nod, she continues, "I was just as devastated as Sylvia when Qasean was killed, we were twins. A part of me died with him, and I threw myself into my cooking while Sylvia decided to go for revenge against those that killed him and the rest of her family. I understand what drives her, she has been in love with my brother since she was fourteen years old, and to have him taken away from her nearly destroyed her. In some ways, I think it has destroyed her, but I can't abandon her now. When I saw the two of you at the restaurant today, I knew I would not be able to stay out of the middle of this, but I refuse to choose between the two of you. If you can't accept my relationship with her, then walk away now. If you are willing to give us a chance, don't expect me to give you information about her nor do I want you giving me information about her. I try to keep myself detached from the things that she does in her quest for revenge, but she has been like my sister since we were fourteen and she's all I have left of Qasean. Unable to help herself, she bursts into tears and turns her back to Quentin.

He comes up behind her, and wraps his arms around her pulling her back against his chest. He holds her until she has no more tears left, then turns her around to face him. He kisses the tears from her face before finding her lips to give her a kiss of comfort and understanding. However, needing to release some tension and emotion, Quintana turns the kiss into a passionate one. Again they make love frantically. When their passion has cooled down, Quentin tilts up her face to his. "I'm sorry I got angry with you. I just didn't know what to think. Sylvia is a renegade according to the government, and I just didn't want to think that you are a part of what she is doing. I would never ask you to betray a trust or a friendship. Please say that you'll forgive me?"

"I'm sorry too. It's just all still so painful for me. Let's just put this behind us, okay?"

"Okay." He pulls her into a tight embrace and they fall asleep that way.

Food From The Heart

Bad Blood

Quentin's alarm goes off as it does every morning at five thirty, and he awakens to the scent of Quintana surrounding him. Deciding that he would rather work out with the woman sleeping in his arms than running his normal five miles, he starts with her eyes and kisses his way down to her throat. When he pulls the sheet down to her waist and begins suckling at her breast, she moans as she opens her eyes to look at the top of his head. He moves to the other breast before working his way down to her hips, and then on to the place he loves kissing as much as he loves kissing her mouth. It doesn't take long for her orgasm to explode inside her like fireworks on the Fourth of July. Before she can even catch her breath, he enters her in one swift thrust that further prevents her from breathing. His loving is as rough as hurricane tossed seas, and she clings to him as though he is the only thing that is preventing her from being sucked up into the eye of the storm. In the end, they are both picked up and tossed about by the waves of pleasure before being washed up on shore trying to catch their breath.

"That was some wake up call," quips Quintana once she is able to breathe normally again.

"It certainly was better than my usual five mile run at the crack of dawn," he replies.

"The crack of dawn," returns Quintana. "Exactly what time is it," she then asks.

He glances at the clock on her nightstand before replying, "Six fifteen."

"Six fifteen," she states at a near yell. "Are you serious?"

"Quite," he responds.

"I'm going back to sleep," she states before burying herself beneath the covers once again.

"I would love to say the same, but I've got to run. Got a long list of things to take care of today." Hmm is all he hears from Quintana as she buries herself deeper under the covers. He chuckles before asking, "Is that your way of saying you're not walking me to the door?"

"You would be correct," she responds while burying deeper still under the covers.

Quentin chuckles as he walks out of the bedroom, and makes his way home to change clothes. After showering and changing clothes, he does another drive through the city looking at vacant lots and abandoned buildings in an effort to maintain his front as a real estate broker. As he pulls up in front of the last property he plans to look at today, who does he see in his rear view mirror? None other than the unconventional Ms Williams.

He steps out of his car and walks towards hers, as she rolls down her window he asks, "Are you following me again Ms Williams?"

"No, but I wonder if it's coincidence that we keep turning up in the same places," she states in a somewhat irate voice.

He keeps his composure, pastes on a smile, and asks, "What is it about me that you don't like?"

Food From The Heart

"I don't like anyone who pretends to be something that they're not," she responds.

"I assure you, Ms Williams, I am a real estate broker. One of the best in the business too I might add."

"You may be that on the surface, but there's more to you than meets the eye and be assured that I will find out what that is," she states as she rolls up her window and puts her car in reverse.

Not wanting to get ran over, he quickly moves out of her way. As he stands in the street watching her drive off, one of the locals walks down the street. "Don't get on her bad side man," the gentleman states. "She's a mean viper who will not hesitate to strike when provoked."

"I don't even know the lady, so I don't know how I can be provoking her. Hell, she's the one who keeps following me around," replies Quentin.

"All I'm a say is, if you're hiding something, she will find out about it." At Quentin's arched brow, the gentleman continues, "My grandson was using his motorcycle garage as a front for some Wall Street type drug dealers, and she found out about all of them including the president of one of the top brokerage firms in this city. She stripped each and everyone one of them of everything but they drawls. All I'm saying is if you got something to hide, stay out of her way if you don't want to suffer the same fate."

As the man continues on down the street, Quentin has another out of place piece of the puzzle that is Sylvia Williams. He makes a mental note to have Brad run down anything that she has even been remotely involved in since she's been in Dallas. He then gets back in his car to head over to his offices to make the call to Brad before he heads over to his condo.

ReGina Crawford

Just as he exits his car with a couple of buckets of paint for his condo, who does he see standing outside his building but the ever lurking Sylvia Williams. "Okay lady, I've had just about enough of your stalking. You need to back off," he states very irritated at this point.

Taken by surprise, Sylvia cocks an eyebrow before stating in a surprisingly calm voice, "I wasn't following you this time. I happen to live in this building. So are you now masquerading as an interior designer so that you can turn the tables on me?"

"Sorry for snapping at you," he replies, "and I happen to have just bought a condo in the building. I'm painting the walls, thus the paint," he continues holding up the buckets in his hands. "I'm normally not this grouchy, it's just been a grueling couple of weeks moving here and trying to get my condo livable and my office workable. I really am sorry for snapping at you," he states again.

"Not a problem. I usually have that effect on people since I tend to rub them the wrong way," she responds around a ghost of a smile.

"You enjoy rubbing people the wrong way." It wasn't really a question, more of a statement really.

"I'm really not into bonding with people, so my technique works for me."

"That seems like it would be a very lonely existence, but you seem to have bonded with Quintana."

He thinks he sees a flash of pain in her eyes before she speaks, but he's not quite sure. "That's different. We became friends when I was different," she states in a somewhat far away voice. However, she quickly regains her composure and adds, "I just hope our paths don't keep crossing like this. It just seems too much of a

Food From The Heart

coincidence." She walks off into the building before Quentin can make heads or tails of this latest encounter.

Revelations II

Deciding that now is not the time to try to figure out the puzzle that is Ms Williams, Quentin heads inside to his condo to begin painting. After getting everything set to go, he decides to turn on the radio for some mood music. Less than thirty minutes into painting, the radio broadcast is interrupted by late breaking news.

'Important News Flash – An abandoned building on the city's south side has just exploded. Firefighters are on the scene, but are having very little success in getting the flames to go out. It seems the blast rocked about two city blocks as the building exploded. We'll keep you updated as more news becomes available.'

"Damn, what the hell is that about," Quentin asks out loud. "Let me call Brad and get him on this in case it has something do with what I'm working on," he continues. However, before he can pick up his phone and dial the number, there's a frantic knock on his door. "Who hell could that be," he asks as he heads to the door. Upon opening the door, he sees a visibly upset Sylvia Williams.

"Okay buster, tell me who you are and tell me now," she states angrily as she pushes past him into the condo.

"Look here Lady, you have no right to come barging in here like this," he responds just as angrily. "Besides what have I done now to have you screaming at me like this?"

Food From The Heart

"I don't know how you know, but you obviously know who I am and what I'm doing, and you're trying to stop me. But blowing up my base of operations will not stop me from completing my mission," she throws at him at the top of her lungs.

"Okay, what kind of drugs are you on? I have no idea what you're talking about."

"The building that is all over the airwaves. The one that just blew up. It was my base of operations," she responds as she continues to look at him as though she is ready to kill him at the slightest provocation.

"The news flash that just came over the radio about the explosion, that's what you're talking about? I have nothing to do with that. I don't know who you are, nor do I care who you are. And frankly, I have had enough of you to last me a lifetime. So please do me a favor, and get the hell out of my home so I can get back to work," he states as he makes a move to reopen the front door.

'Important update – It seems the explosion was a miniature bomb set off to be a warning as the firefighters discover a message carved into the only wall left standing after the blast. 'We know who you are Ms Williams. Back-off or you'll meet the same fate as your family' is the message that was left. The FBI and CIA have been called in to try to figure out who this Ms Williams is, and who wants her dead. Stay tuned for further updates.'

"Okay Lady, that's it. Like I said, I don't know who you are, and I'm convinced more now than ever that I don't want to know who you are. If someone is trying to kill you, I don't want them to think that I know anything about you and what you are doing. Now, get out," he shouts as he opens the door.

"Look, I'm sor . . . ," Sylvia begins.

"Save it Lady, and just get out," he states in a very angry voice. Sylvia drops her head, and walks out the door. Quentin slams the door behind her, and takes a seat in the middle of the floor. Before he can even get his thoughts in order, his phone rings. "Yeah," he barks.

"Whoa," states Brad on the other end. "What the hell bit you in the ass?"

"Sorry man. Some weird shit just happened here. I was trying to get myself together before giving you a call."

"That's exactly what I'm calling you about. The building was being used by Ms Sylvia Williams as her base of operations, and the bomb that blew it up has the same signature as bombs used in the past by a guy who uses the code name Mr. Red."

"Shit! Shit! And more shit," hisses Quentin.

"What," shouts Brad into the phone.

"Remember the conversation that I overheard when I first got here," asks Quentin.

"Yeah, what about it?"

"Mr. Red was paying someone to scare someone else. I wonder if the person he was talking about is Ms Williams."

"Shit! Shit! And more shit," shouts Brad on the other end of the line.

"Exactly," shouts Quentin.

"Okay, let me put some things in motion regarding Ms Williams, and see what information I can find on this Mr. Red since no one

Food From The Heart

seems to know his true identity. I'll get back to you when I have more info." The line goes dead.

Quentin spends another ten minutes on the floor before grabbing his keys, and heading over to his office to do some research on his own. He has some connections of his own that he only uses under extreme circumstances, and he considers this to be extreme circumstances.

*****

Once in the office, Quentin switches the chip I his phone and places a call. When the phone is answered, he states "Lion Hunter here."

"Jackal," states the voice on the other end.

"News flash. Dallas. Details," states Quentin.

"Peace time tomorrow," states the voice before the line goes dead.

Quentin changes the chip in his phone, and fires up his computer to begin searching the internet for information on what happened to Sylvia's family. After three longs hours in front of the screen, he finally finds some information buried beneath tons of red tape.

Apparently Sylvia and her team, where in hot pursuit of one of the biggest illegal gunners in history when their cover was blown, and everyone on the team was assassinated. Sylvia was spared because the men in her unit decided not to inform her of their plans, and executed a sting without her knowledge and consent. They drugged her and left her behind in their safe house, unaware that they were walking into an ambush. The team took the true identity of who they were after to the grave with them, so Sylvia has dedicated her life to finding out his true identity and bringing him to justice.

Quentin wonders if Mr. Red is the person he is chasing; who he really is; and will he be able to bring him down before Sylvia ends up dead. Knowing there is nothing more that he can do at the moment, he heads to his sister's house for some much needed rest. He'll just have to wait for the update from the Jackal tomorrow.

Food From The Heart

Peace Time

Quentin has a difficult time focusing as he waits for the information that the Jackal can find, and it seems as though the clock on the wall is moving in slow motion. As time seems to move slower and slower and his concentration seems to be getting fuzzier and fuzzier, Quentin decides to leave his office, and go finish the painting at his condo that he failed to finish yesterday.

Just as he his pulling up in front of the building, he sees Sylvia loading luggage into the trunk of her car, and thinks to himself *'Good move lady. Go underground for a while so I can find out what's really going on.'* He doesn't look her way as he is getting out of his car, then heads straight for the front door of the condo building.

Sylvia sees Quentin pull up to the building, but doesn't stop loading her luggage. *'I wonder if he will stop and say anything to me before going inside'*, she thinks to herself. As he makes his way inside the building without so much as a glance in her direction, she further thinks, *'I guess he wasn't joking when he said he doesn't want anyone to think that he knows me. Maybe I'm wrong about him. Maybe he's not more than he appears to be.'* She shakes her head as if to clear it, *'I can't start doubting myself now. I've got too much invested in this,"* she whispers to herself. After loading her luggage, she gets in her car to head to parts unknown while she tries to figure out who has found out about her, and how they found out about her.

Once inside his condo, Quentin peeks through the blinds just in time to see Sylvia pull off and to see the car that pulls off behind her. He quickly jots down the license plate number to see if he can find out who's tailing her. He needs to get a handle on all the players, and quick.

He pulls out his phone to call Brad to give him the plate number. It takes Brad less than ten seconds to tell him that the car tailing Sylvia is one of theirs. They want to keep an eye on her in case there are any more threats sent her way. The agency wants to know what happened to Sylvia's team as much as Sylvia does.

After ending the call with Brad, Quentin changes clothes, and begins painting to work off some of the aggravation that he is feeling. Four hours later, he is pleased with the progress that he has made with the condo. After taking a shower, he changes the chip in his phone so that he may receive the call from the Jackal.

> *Peace Time: In Ottawa, Canada the Peace Tower located at the House of Parliament houses one of that country's most famous clocks. On May 28, 2006 the clock inexplicably stopped working for one day, displaying the time of 7:28 to the confusion of many, sparking news stories often called the day that time stood still.*

At exactly seven twenty-eight his phone rings, and he knows who the caller is on the other end. He answers, "Lion Hunter."

"Jackal," is the response from the other end.

"Details," responds Quentin.

Food From The Heart

"Explosive material contains the same signature as the material that killed a combat unit that was about to bring down a major illegal arms operation. Ms Williams is the only surviving member of that unit, and has dedicated her life to finding the man responsible. No identity on Mr. Red or what his connection is to either bombing. It seems he has a great plastic surgeon that keeps changing his identity every six months, and he changes team members even more frequently although no one knows what happens to the team members he releases. Theory is that they are fertilizer somewhere. Bone fragments have been found near reported safe houses, but there has never been enough to identify who they belong to. Advice stay clear. Peace time two days." The report is given, and the line goes dead.

Quentin is more determined than ever to solve this mystery after receiving the report, but knows that he must do so as the invisible man. He changes the chip in his phone, before heading to Quintana's restaurant for dinner and hopefully some dessert.

He arrives at the restaurant, and is immediately shown to "his" table near the kitchen. After looking over the menu, Quentin orders dinner and waits for Quintana to find out he's there. She arrives at his table shortly after his order is placed. As she approaches him, he flashes her his irresistible smile that shows off his dimples. "Hello gorgeous," he states when she stops in front of him.

"Hello handsome," she responds. "What are you up to?"

"Whatever do you mean? I'm just having dinner," he quips around the smile he's trying desperately to hide.

"You know exactly what I mean. Why did every dish you ordered have some type of aphrodisiac in it?"

"They did," he asks trying to appear as though he wasn't aware of that fact.

"They did, and you very well know it. So what are you up to?"

"Just want to make sure that I'm up to giving a special lady everything she wants and desires."

"I don't think you need any help in that area, but we'll put it to the test later," she states as she winks at him before turning to head back to the kitchen. "Enjoy your meal," she throws over her shoulder as she walks through the kitchen doors.

Quentin laughs as she disappears, then sits back to await his meal.

*****

When Quintana arrives at home that night, she finds her living room turned into a fantasy come true. There are candles in every corner of the room giving off the scent of vanilla, all of the furniture has been moved into the dining room, the floor is covered with a giant pillow that resembles an Indian Carpet, and there are all types of oils in a warmer next to a lounging Quentin. "Welcome home Princess. Your bath is ready and waiting. You've got twenty minutes, and then I'm coming to get you."

Quintana lifts her eyebrow in challenge before smiling, and heading to the waiting bath. Quintana undresses, and enjoys the soothing effects of the bath for fifteen minutes before bathing with the soap she finds waiting for her. Without benefit of drying off, she returns to her living room to find Quentin leaning against her mantel completely naked and ready for action. They begin walking in each other's direction to only meet up in the middle of the pillow that will serve as their bed for the evening.

Quentin proceeds to lick the moisture from her skin as he lowers her to the pillow. Before long Quintana is overwhelmed by the skill of Quentin's tongue and lips, and begins moaning out her enjoyment. "It's too early for that baby, I haven't even gotten started yet," he

Food From The Heart

whispers between kisses to her flesh. To prove his point, he slides his head between her legs and begins to enjoy the dessert his been waiting hours to enjoy.

At her climax, Quintana screams his name at the top of her lungs, but that doesn't stop Quentin from over indulging and he brings her to another climax with his lips and tongue. Before she can fully recover from her first two orgasms, Quentin quickly enters her hot wet cove and loves her through three more orgasms before he finds his own release. They fall into an exhausted sleep in each other's arms.

ReGina Crawford

Peace Time II

For the next two days, Quentin resumes his regular routine scouting property and making connections as a Real Estate Broker not trying to give away his anxiousness while waiting to hear back from Brad and the Jackal.

At one o'clock on day two, he receives a call from Brad. "What do you have for me," asks Quentin upon answering the phone.

"Hello to you too. Things are great here in the office, thanks for asking," responds Brad sarcastically.

"Sorry man. This case has more twists and turns than a Sidewinder, and I'm a little on edge."

"No problem. You need to relax a little though. Don't want you blowing your cover."

"Not likely. I am the best at camouflage when in the public eye, and you know it. That's why you sent me here."

"True dat. True dat," replies Brad. "Here's the update. Sylvia is holed up in a very secure location that cannot be tied back to her or to us. She has twenty-four hour surveillance that not even she can shake, so no need to worry about her for the moment. I'll let you know when she comes from under her rock. As for Mr. Red, he

Food From The Heart

seems to be a chameleon when it comes to changing his identity. I have sent you some photos of men suspected of being him, see if you can meld them together to find common features to see if it is indeed the same person in all of the photos. We also have his known hideouts under surveillance to see who comes and goes. I'll send you the footage as soon as I get it."

"Thanks man. I should be fully operational in a couple of weeks, and I'll keep you updated as I gather information."

"Good," responds Brad before ending the call.

Quentin gathers the photos, and begins processing them through the software that he helped developed. Several hours later he feels he has several key features identified about the identity of Mr. Red. Now all he has to do is gather photos of the key players in the area and do a similar comparison.

Once that's complete, Quentin does some research on top plastic surgeons around the world to try to pinpoint which of them could possibly be on Mr. Red's payroll. Once he's pinpointed the top five surgeons in the world, he begins digging into their finances to see where their money is coming from. Unfortunately, his research finds nothing out of the ordinary in their finances. So, if any of them are on Mr. Red's payroll, they're hiding the money very well or their payments are something other than monetary in any shape, form, or fashion.

Once completing his research, Quentin takes note of the time, and switches the chip in his phone so that he can receive the second update from the Jackal.

The phone rings at exactly seven twenty-eight. Quentin answers, "Lion Hunter."

"Jackal."

"Updates."

"Ms Williams has definitely made some enemies in the illegal arms trade. She has confiscated shipments, replaced live ammunition with fake ammunition. Just been a real pain in the ass, so they are really gunning for her. No updates on Mr. Red or his associates."

"Details," responds Quentin. "Dr.'s Nickels, Abernathy, Castellanos, Yamamoto, Lombardi."

"Peace Time. Two days." Again the line goes dead.

Quentin closes up his office, and once again heads over to Quintana's to prepare her a special evening when she gets off work. This time the set up resembles a Hawaiian get away.

When Quintana arrives home, her breath is taken away by the scene that Quentin has created. As she makes her way to the bathroom for her bath she asks Quentin, "How do you manage to turn my house into these fantastic fantasies?"

"If I tell you, I'll have to kill you," quips Quentin around his laughter.

"Hell, you're killing me anyway."

"But at least this way, you'll die with a smile on your face."

Quintana laughs out loud as she removes her clothing, and gets into her waiting bath.
After the thorough loving that Quentin gives her, Quintana is out like a light. But Quentin has too much on his mind to sleep, so he lays there holding her thinking. How does he close this case and keep Sylvia alive? It's a good thing that she has gone underground, and he hopes that she stays there until the case is resolved. Which of the surgeons is on Mr. Red's payroll? And just who the hell is Mr.

Food From The Heart

Red? Deciding that he will not receive any answers to his questions tonight, he pulls Quintana closer and closes his eyes to get some sleep.

Two days later at peace time, Quentin is awaiting the updates from the Jackal. "Lion Hunter," states Quentin when he answers the phone.

"Jackal," replies the voice on the other end. "Yamamoto and Lombardi are the ones to watch. Yamamoto was convicted of crimes against the Japanese government, but managed to disappear before his death sentence could be carried out. His family doesn't appear to be affected by this, so payments for his services may be going directly to the Japanese government so that his family will be left alone and that is why you see nothing odd in his financial records. Lombardi is a big gambler and while his debts haven't been completely wiped clean, his family doesn't appear to be suffering any consequences either."

The line goes dead, and Quentin feels slightly better knowing he has some possible leads as to who can be helping Mr. Red keep his identity a secret.

ReGina Crawford

Open for Business

After two more weeks of work, Quentin's condo is finally ready for him to move into, and he and Quintana waste no time christening every inch of the place. He has not seen hide nor hair of Ms Williams since the day she loaded her luggage in her car, and he hopes that she keeps a low profile until the mystery of her family's deaths can be solved.

Two days after his condo is complete, his offices are also ready to be opened and he is ready to get down to the business he was sent here to handle. During the day he power sells his skills to investors and builders alike, and at night he power sells a whole other set of skills to Quintana. His business takes off without a hitch, and his relationship with his woman becomes stronger and stronger as days turn into weeks, and weeks turn into months.

Finally, after three months of power plays, Quentin meets the men who are the reason for his front as a real estate broker. They walk into his office looking like legitimate investors with their Italian Silk Suits, tasteful yet expensive looking jewelry, and no noticeable glock bulges under their jackets.

"Good afternoon gentlemen," greets Quentin. "Please come in and have a seat. Can I get you anything – coffee, water, soft drink, brandy?"

Food From The Heart

"Good afternoon Mr. McNair," greets the man whom Quentin assumes is the top man of the organization as he nods his head to the other gentlemen to take a position behind the seats at the conference table. "I am Charles Givens, and these are my associates Marcus Henderson, Jason Lewis, and Frank Jackson." The men shake hands before taking their seats.

"It's a pleasure to meet all of you," states Quentin as he dims the light and starts the presentation on the wall monitor. "In front of each of you is a folder with the details of the proposal that you are here to consider investing in," he begins as the first slide appears on the screen. "As you will see this project has been well thought out and well planned, and I can't see it being anything but a success," he continues as he shows them pictures of the land in question followed by the mock designs for the business center that his architect has put together. Once all of the financial documents have been reviewed, Quentin makes his final pitch. "Although the area where the business center will be built is considered poverty stricken, there are a lot entrepreneurs in that area that will greatly benefit from the business center and they will help ensure its success."

"Very impressive," states Charles Givens. "I must admit I was extremely skeptical about this proposal prior to your presentation, but you have made a believer out of me. However, I still would like some additional time to review the proposal with my attorney and financial advisors prior to committing to investing in this project."

"Of course. That is completely understandable," responds Quentin.

"Great," replies Givens, "I will be back in contact with you within a week to inform you of my decision."

"That is fine with me, and I would like to thank each of you for taking the time to meet with me today," states Quentin as he extends his hand to each of them.

ReGina Crawford

After he is sure that they have traveled a good distance from his office, Quentin locks the front door and enters the secret room off of his supply closet. He calls headquarters on the secure line that they have installed to see what his boss has to say about the meeting. "Brad, Q here," he states when the phone is answered.

"Really," states Brad sarcastically since it could be no one else on the other end of the line.

"Don't be sarcastic Brad," states Quentin with laughter in his voice. "I've got some video footage I'm about to send to you from my meeting today. Let me know as soon as you have any info on them. In the meantime, I will run the picture of Mr. Givens through my software to see if he has any of the same features as the elusive Mr. Red"

"Sure thing. Send it on over. Let me know if you find any similarities."

Quentin sends the footage, and then proceeds to unlock his front door once again deciding he will wait till later this evening to run the picture of Mr. Givens through his software. As he re-opens the blinds, who does he see standing outside his door? None other than Ms Sylvia Williams with a huge frown on her face. He opens the door, "Good afternoon, Ms Williams, I haven't seen you for quite a while. Thought you had left the city."

"I bet," she states sarcastically as she walks through the door. Once Quentin has closed the door, she spins on him and starts firing questions at him. "Why were you meeting with Charles Givens and his crew? Why did you lock your office door after they left? I know I've asked this before but just who are you? And why are you in my city?"

Surprised and angered by the venom in her voice, Quentin barks back just as harshly as he approaches her, "I don't know who you

Food From The Heart

think you are and why you feel you have the right to barge into my office and question me about anything. I don't have to answer to you, and I trust that you will remember that in the future." He is now standing nose-to-nose with her, and both are shooting daggers at each other with their eyes. "Besides shouldn't you be more concerned about who's trying to kill you?"

Not the least bit intimated by his size or his anger, Sylvia stands her ground, "I would like answers to my questions, and I want them now."

Not willing to back down either, Quentin answers, "Who I have meetings with is none of your business. Why I close my office is none of your business. As I've said before, my name is Quentin McNair and I'm a real estate broker here to do business in real estate. That's what real estate brokers do." He then heads to the door and opens it as he says, "Good day Ms Williams."

Walking in the direction of the open door, Sylvia states, "I will get answers to my questions one way or the other."

"I wish you the best of luck with that," he states while still holding the door open.

Walking out the door, Sylvia states, "This is not over."

Quentin doesn't say another word as he closes the door behind her. "That woman is working my last nerve. I need to call Brad and see if he can do something about her." He places the call to Brad, before finishing up the rest of the paper work sitting on his desk.

ReGina Crawford

Unanswered Questions

With his mood resembling a thunder storm after the encounter with
Sylvia, Quentin decides to close his office for the day, and run the
photos of Charles Givens through his software program. The results
are inclusive. While there were a few similarities between the photo
of Charles and the ones that are reported to be of Mr. Red, there are
just aren't enough similarities to say that they are one and the same.
Once his work is done for the day, Quentin heads home to his condo
to change clothes for his evening workout. Once he leaves the gym,
he heads over to Quintana's to wait for her to get off work.
However, when he arrives he notices that her place has been broken
into, so he calls his brother-in-law Kyle and sits outside in his car to
wait for his arrival.

In less than twenty minutes, both Kyle and Keith arrive at
Quintana's. Kyle and Keith enter the house ahead of Quentin with
their guns drawn. They search the entire house, but there is no one
inside. However, they do notice that her office has been gone
through very thoroughly.

As Kyle and Keith holster their guns, they ask, "Who would be
looking for something in here?"

"I don't know," answers Quentin. "I would find it very strange if
any other restaurant owners would be willing to break into here."

Food From The Heart

"Yes, that would be strange," replies Kyle as he puts on gloves to begin looking through all the papers on the desk. "All I see are accounting records for the business, but that information is not going to help her competition."

Keith, who is looking at Quintana's laptop sitting on the other end of the desk, states, "Maybe they weren't looking for information on Quintana or her restaurant." As Kyle and Quentin swing their heads in his direction, he continues, "It seems whoever was here was looking for information on Quentin." He then turns the laptop in their direction, and they see that the would be thief left a search screen open on the screen that has Quentin's name in it.

"Now who would be looking for information on you here at Quintana's," asks Kyle while looking at Quentin.

"Quintana is not involved in my business. She hasn't even been to my office, so the people I'm doing business with shouldn't even know about her."

"You sure you haven't been under surveillance by anyone you've been doing business with," asks Keith.

Quentin gives him an *are-you-serious* look before rolling his eyes. "The only person who has been dogging me is Ms Williams, but she and Quintana are like family. She wouldn't break in here, especially to look for information on me." At Kyle and Keith's skeptical looks, he adds "The woman is a pro. If she wanted to come in here and look for information on me, she wouldn't have left any evidence that anyone was here."

"Then who would have done this," ask Kyle.

"I don't know, but they must have gotten scared to leave that search screen up."

"You don't think they were in here while you were outside do you," asks Keith.

"I guess it's possible," replies Quentin, "but they didn't come out the front door or I would have seen them. Plus I saw no cars move while I was waiting for you."

"Well I'm calling forensics and have them dust the place. Although I'm not too optimistic about them finding any prints," states Kyle.

Quintana arrives home to find the place filled with officers, and is livid after the long day that she had today. "What the hell is going on here," she asks as she walks through the door.

Quentin quickly walks over to her to explain, "When I got here your door was broken in. I called Kyle, and he and Keith came over to investigate. When we found your office had been searched, they called forensics to see if they could get any information on who broke in here."

"Why would anyone want to break in here," she asks shaking. "I don't have anything that anyone would want to steal."

"I don't think they were here to steal anything sweetheart. There was a search screen on your laptop when we got in here." At her questioning look, he continues, "They were searching for documents with my name attached."

"Why would anyone be looking for documents on my laptop that have anything to do with you? We aren't in the same business. We don't even do business together."

"I know sweetheart. I don't know why this happened."

Needing time to think, Quintana asks, "How much longer are they going to be?"

Food From The Heart

"They shouldn't be too much longer."

"I'll be in the kitchen until they finish. Please let me know once everyone has left." As she turns to leave, Quentin reaches for her and she jumps back. At his questioning look, she states, "I need a minute to process this. Just let me know when they are done." She turns and walks from the room.

Ten minutes later, the forensics team is done processing everything and they along with Kyle and Keith leave Quentin and Quintana alone. Quentin enters the kitchen, and finds Quintana sitting at the table drinking a cup of tea. "Everyone's gone sweetheart." At the look of anguish on her face, he adds, "Let's go start your bath, and then we can talk."

"I don't know if it's a good idea for you to stay here tonight under the circumstances," states Quintana as she gets up and places her cup in the sink.

"I don't agree with you. Someone broke in here tonight. I don't think you should be here alone."

"I'm not trying to be difficult, but I need to process all that has happened and I won't be able to do that with you here."

"Are you blaming me for this? Is that why you're asking me to leave," questions Quentin as he stares her directly in the eye.

"To be honest, I'm not sure. But I do know that right now, at this very moment, I need space to think. If it's not safe for me to stay here, then I'll go stay at a hotel."

"If you don't want me with you, then I would feel better if you stayed at a hotel instead of here," responds Quentin.

"Fine. I'll pack a bag and stay at the Wyndham," replies Quintana as she heads to her bedroom to pack a bag. When she returns to the living room, Quentin is sitting on the couch with his head laid back and his eyes closed. She could see the lines of strain on his forehead and around his mouth. She quietly states, "I'm ready." At the look of pain in his eyes when he opens them, she adds, "I'm not trying to punish you for this. I just need a minute to wrap my head around this. It takes me back to when Qasean was killed, and I've found that I have some feelings from that I haven't dealt with. And I need to think, and you dominant my thoughts when you're with me. Please tell me you understand?"

At the anguish in her voice, he relents, "I understand sweetheart. Just know that if you find that you need me at anytime, all you have to do is call and I'll be there in a heartbeat." He notices the breath that she releases, and realizes that she had been holding her breath waiting for his response. This further weakens his anger, and he pulls her into his arms. She comes willingly, and wraps her arms tightly around his waist. "It's okay baby. I'll always be here for you whenever you need me, and I'll always give you space when you need it. Always remember that." He feels her nodding her head yes against his chest. "Come on, let's get you to the Wyndham."

They walk out the door to their respective cars and after getting her checked into the Wyndham, Quentin heads home to his condo.

Food From The Heart

Searching For Answers

Once Quintana is in her room, she takes a long hot shower before sitting down on the bed to think. What happened today has her replaying all the events from the death of her brother, and has her thinking that the events of the past are tied to today's events. "I need answers," she says out loud to herself, "and I know just where to start." She searches her purse for her cell phone, and upon finding it punches in the number of her best friend.

The phone rings three times before it's picked up. "Hello," answers the voice on the other end of the phone.

"I need you to be straight with me," responds Quintana.

"I'm always straight with you," says the voice on the other end of the phone with some irritation. "What is this about?"

"I need to know what you know about the break-in at my home tonight."

"Why would I know anything about it?"

"Sylvia, don't bullshit me. I want answers and I want them now."

"Alright Ana, your boy is meeting with some heavy hitters from the underground, and I need to know what he's up to. And I will find out what he's up to whether you and he want me to or not."

"Why is that so important to you? And why are you willing to put me in the middle of it? I thought that we were closer than that."

"Ana, you know you mean the world to me. You are all that I have left of my life with Qasean, and I would never do anything to intentionally hurt you. But I know that you and your boy are keeping something from me, and you know that I am like a dog with a bone when it comes to stuff like this. I can't let it go even if it brings tension between the two of us, but I do know that our bond is strong enough to endure this just as we have endured in the past."

"Sylvia, I wish you would let go of all the anger and pain you are still feeling after all these years. I think that the pain of the day we lost Q is clouding your brain, and it is turning you into a very bitter person. I love you and I will always love you, but as in the past I will not get caught up in this game of danger and intrigue that you are playing. I just want to know one thing, why did you make it look like a regular burglary? I know how good you are, and you could have come into my home and no one would have been the wiser."

"It's very simple really. If I did find something out about him, I had planned to leak the information to the underground, the media, and law enforcement, and when that happened I wanted him to think that one of the people he is in bed with leaked the information. If he's undercover which I truly believe he is, he probably knows all about me and would have figured out that I was the one that leaked the information."

"Let me state this one more time, there is nothing to find out about Quentin. He has nothing to do with the people that you are searching for, and I don't know why you won't let it go. I do not want to be a pawn in the middle between you, and I don't appreciate you involving me in this."

Food From The Heart

"Ana I'm not trying to upset you, but there is more to your boy than you want to believe. And you know I can't let this go, there is no reason that Q should have died the way that he did not to mention the rest of my family."

Cutting Sylvia off, Quintana interjects, "It was their time to go, accept it and move on. I have, and it's time that you did too. You don't know how much you've changed over the years Sylvia, and to be honest you're starting to scare me."

With irritation in her voice, Sylvia responds, "Fine Ana. Live your life how you see fit, and I'll do the same. Talk to you later." Sylvia hangs up the phone leaving Quintana staring at her cell phone like it had suddenly morphed into some alien creature. Not willing to let herself get more upset than she already is, Quintana sets the phone down on the desk and decides to fire up the Jacuzzi since the tension released by her earlier shower has returned.

*****

Quentin arrives home and immediately makes some calls to a few higher ups that owe him a favor or two. He knows in his gut that Sylvia was behind the break-in at Quintana's, and wants more information on her. He knows that the agency has to be keeping close tabs on her movements and contacts since they want to know what happened all those years ago as well.

Twenty minutes later his phone is ringing displaying a familiar number, and he immediately picks it up. "Black Mambo here," he answers.

"Dirt Doctor. Is this line secure," comes the response from the other end.

"Yes. Lockjaw in place," responds Q.

ReGina Crawford

"Been waiting on your call. It seems that the people on your tape Snake Chaser has been monitoring for over a year due to a connection they have with her number one suspect in the death of her family. She is the one behind the break-in, and she is worse than a dog with a meaty bone once she sinks her teeth. And her teeth are embedded tightly in this one. My advice to you is to be four times as careful as you have ever been. We're monitoring her, and will try to keep her off your ass a much as possible but she's as cunning as her name. Dirt Doctor out." And the line goes dead.

"Shit, I need more information than that," states Quentin out loud before placing a call to Brad. The line is picked up after the second ring. "What you got for me," he asks.

"It's not good. The three gentlemen that you met with are on the top of Sylvia's hit list, and your association with them adds you to that list. The woman is ruthless, and doesn't give a damn about innocent by-standers when it comes to getting what she's after. And the fact that she doesn't consider you an innocent by-stander makes you a heavier target in her book."

"Damn. I need to know why her team set up that sting without her. No one knows what made them walk into that ambush?"

"Not that I know of. I can try to find out what I can, but it will take a minute," replies Brad. "Stay by the phone. I'll call you back when I have more info." The line goes dead.

"This is not how this was supposed to go down," states Quentin to his empty condo. Frustrated beyond belief, he heads over to his newly acquired workout equipment in an attempt to relieve some of his frustrations.

Food From The Heart

New Development

The week that Charles Givens requested has come and gone, and Quentin hasn't heard back from him. Nor has he spent any time with Quintana since he agreed to give her the space that she needed. Ms Williams has also kept her distance, which makes Quentin suspicious as hell as to what she is up to. Quentin's frustration level is at the highest it's ever been, but he knows he must maintain his composure so that he doesn't give anyone an advantage in this snake pit he has found himself in.

Friday afternoon seems to be taking forever to pass as Quentin watches the clock on the wall, hoping that someone makes contact with him today. Just as he is about to make a fresh pot of coffee, the monitor on his desk shows him that Mr. Givens and his crew have just arrived. Not wanting to give away his monitoring system, Quentin proceeds to the coffee pot and begins making a fresh pot just as Charles and his crew walk through the door.

Turning at the sound of the door chime, Quentin pastes a fake, yet believable, smile on his face and greets his guests. "Good afternoon Mr. Givens, gentlemen," he states as they all file through the door.

"Good afternoon Mr. McNair," they all state at once.

"Please have a seat. I was just making a fresh pot of coffee. It should be ready shortly."

"Great. I've met with my attorneys and advisors, and they seem to believe in your project as well. So, I am willing to make a substantial investment into this project."

"I promise you, you will not regret your decision," states Quentin around his award winning smile as he reaches around the desk to shake hands with Charles Givens.

"How soon will you be able to get a contract together for my team and I to review?"

"As soon as you get me any must haves for the contract, I will get that information over to our attorneys, and then the contracts should be ready in a week."

"Great. We'll be awaiting the contracts, and will get them back to you as soon as possible," states Charles as he stands.

"I'll messenger them to you as soon as they are ready," states Quentin as he too stands and shakes hands with the gentlemen.

After the gentlemen leave, Quentin's spirits are boosted and he begins making plans to keep tabs on every movement made by Charles and his associates from this point on.

*****

By the close of business, Quentin is confident that the plans he has made will help bring an end to this case as soon as the development is complete. However, he wants to cover all his bases, so he placed a few more calls.

His first call is answered, but nothing is said by the party on the other end. So Quentin speaks first, "Black Mambo. Lockjaw in place."

Food From The Heart

"Dirt Doctor. Secure," is the response from the other end.

"Anything new," asks Quentin.

"Someone in your camp is not who they appear to be. Evidence of sweeper tactics found, and unaccountable funds transfers. Cleaner team in place if you need it."

"Damn," Quentin spits through clenched teeth. "Vacation cleaners for now. Too many unanswered questions, need to analyze the dust. Heat Seek my camp, and let me know what you find."

"Done. Dirt Doctor out."

The line goes dead, and Quentin doesn't even waste time pondering who in his camp is on the fence. He needs to get these latest developments to the Jackal.

As peace time draws near, Quentin switches the chip in his phone hoping that the Jackal has been keeping tabs on everything, and has an update for him.

When the phone rings, Quentin answers it on the first ring, "Lion Hunter."
"Jackal," responds the voice on the other end of the line.

"Developments. Charles Givens has decided to be an investor in my development. I have already set up surveillance on him and his team, but I need surveillance on the surveillance team since we don't know how high up his connections go. Initiated Heat Seeker on my camp as evidence of double dipping has surfaced. Updates."

"Done. Yamamoto and Lombardi are working together, and have invented a new procedure to alter the appearance of the underlying bone structure of a person's face. Mr. Red may be the first person to benefit from this new procedure, so he indeed may be your Charles Givens. It's good that you are being extra cautious in dealing with him. Ms Williams is back in business as well, so be extra cautious whenever you encounter her. She has a new base of operations, and a new batch of counter-intelligence folks working for her. Not sure where her funding is coming from, but she certainly has unlimited resources. Trying to get a handle on it. Will let you know if I find out anything new."

"That confirms the info I got from the Dirt Doctor," states Quentin just as the line goes dead. "Dammit," he shouts in a whisper. "This is the last thing I need. Someone helping Sylvia. Who could be helping her," he asks himself. After a few more minutes of pondering, he decides that he is not going to give himself a headache trying to figure it out. He trusts the Jackal and the Dirt Doctor to get a handle on it, and he will just continue with his plans. "Let the chips fall where they may," he says before closing his office for the day.

Food From The Heart

Tense Moment

The day for Indigo and Kyle's wedding arrives, and Quentin is more nervous than the groom and it has nothing to do with the actual ceremony. He hasn't seen or talked to Quintana in two weeks, and he's not sure what her reaction will be when she sees him today. Hell, he isn't even sure what his reaction will be to seeing her.

He puts on his best poker face throughout the ceremony, pictures, and limo ride to the reception. However, the moment he steps out of the limo, he feels the sweat forming on his body as he knows that he will be seeing Quintana at any moment. He takes his seat at the head table, and remains as calm as possible while the rest of the guests file in and take their seats. He starts to relax more and more as time goes on and Quintana doesn't make an appearance at the event, and then it happens. Quintana escorts the cake into the room. His heart starts racing, his palms get sweaty, and a huge lump forms in his throat. He takes a sip of champagne but can't seem to get it to go down, and starts joking and coughing. Quintana instantly looks in his direction which only makes him cough even more. He sees the longing and the pain in her eyes, and it only increases his own.

Quintana tried her best not to look at Quentin when she entered the room, but when he started coughing she couldn't help herself. Oh how she has missed that man, but he hasn't tried to contact her in two weeks and it hurts. Listening to her pride, she looks away after looking into his eyes for a minute, and continues setting up the cake.

ReGina Crawford

The moment her task is complete, she makes a bee-line for the kitchen before she breaks down and goes to him.

Once back in the kitchen, Quintana rests her forehead against the refrigerator door as she tries to compose herself after her brief encounter with Quentin. Once her hands stop shaking, she organizes the servers to begin serving the head table. When one of them asks if she's okay, she simply nods her head and begins leading the procession out of the kitchen. Quentin excuses himself from the table and heads for the men's room, where he splashes water on his face to regain his composure. Once he feels in control again, he takes his seat back at the head table. Kyle, Keith, and Kendrick give him a questioning look as he picks up his champagne glass and downs the contents. His answering look says not now, and he signals the server to refill his glass.

As the salads are placed in front of each of the members of the wedding party, neither Quentin nor Quintana make eye contact with each other which is not missed by Indigo, Jade, Ebony, Kyle, Keith, or Kendrick. However, each of them know that now is not the time to say anything to Quentin or Quintana, but once the dancing begins that's another story. It's a few hours later after the meal has been served, the toasts made, that the dancing begins. Since Indigo and Kyle are busy on the dance floor, Keith and Kendrick unassumingly usher Quentin into the back hallway to find out what is going on.

"What's up with you two," asks Quentin once they out of ear shot of the wedding guests.

"What's up with you," is the question both Keith and Kendrick ask at the same time.

"More to the point, what is up with you and Ana," asks Keith.

"What are you blabbing about," asks Quentin.

Food From The Heart

"Don't insult my intelligence by acting like you don't know what I'm talking about," responds Keith. "I've been on the force too long not to notice when people are not acting like themselves. So tell me what's going on."

"I haven't seen her since the night her house was broken into. Hell man, I haven't even talked to her since that night."

"What," shout Keith and Kendrick at the same time. At the look on Quentin's face they know they were kind of loud, so they lower their voices. "Why the hell not?"

"Are you guys working in tandem? What's with the interrogation in stereo," asks Quentin. "Can you appoint one of you as spokesman so that I don't feel like this conversation is taking place in surround sound?"

"Just answer the question," asks Keith.

"When I dropped her off at the hotel, she said she needed space, so I was giving it to her. I figured she would call me when she wanted to talk, and I haven't heard from her. I just didn't think that seeing her here today would be this hard."

"From where I was sitting, it didn't look like it was too easy for her to see you either," states Kendrick. "So what do you plan to do?"

"What do you mean, what do I plan to do?"

"It was a very simple question that I'm sure that you understood," states Keith.
"I don't plan to do anything. She asked for space, and I'm giving it to her." At there *are-you-serious* look, he asks, "What do you suggest I do?"

"We suggest that after this shindig is over, you go talk to the woman," states Keith the self-appointed spokesman. He then looks at Kendrick and says, "Young'ns. Don't know nothing."

"You said it man," responds Kendrick as they both turn away to walk back into the reception hall.

Quentin stays behind contemplating his next move. "The hell with them," he states before returning to the reception himself even though he knows that he will probably follow their advice.

When he reenters the room, Indigo grabs him and leads him to the dance floor. "Okay boy, what the hell is going on?"

"You and your new husband need to keep your minds focused on your new marriage, and off me."

"Don't be a smart-ass boy, or I will have my new husband kick your ass for making me upset on my wedding day. Now tell me what is going on with you and Quintana."

"Nothing is going on with me and Quintana. She asked for space, and I'm giving it to her. End of story."

"That was two weeks ago. Please don't tell me that you haven't reached out to her in all this time." When he doesn't respond, she accidently on purpose steps on his foot.

"Shit," responds Quentin, "What did you do that for?"

"To wake you up. You will go and talk to her after the reception," states Indigo before walking off the dance floor into her husband's waiting arms.

Food From The Heart

Reunion

Two days after the reception, Quentin decides that he's waited long enough to talk to Quintana, and goes to her restaurant hoping that she will talk to him. On the drive there, he's talking out loud to himself. *'I know she was upset about the break-in at her home, but that wasn't my fault. I agreed to give her some space, but two weeks is too damn long to be without her. But the way she disappeared after the reception . . .'* As he enters the restaurant, the hostess practically runs to greet him, "I'm so glad to see you. Life has been hell around here the last two weeks. Let me show you to your table."

Quentin raises his eyebrows at her as she practically drags him to his table. "Lisa, slow down," he states as he lengthens his stride to keep up with her. "What has been going on?"

"The boss has been a bear for the past two weeks. Where have you been," she asks as he takes his seat.

"She asked me for space, so I was giving it to her," he replies.

"Well if you ask me, you gave her too much space. Please don't ever give her this much space again," Lisa states as she walks away to greet the latest guests that have arrived at the restaurant.

Quentin opens his menu, but before he has a chance to even glance at it a hand snatches it from his grasp. He looks up into the eyes of

ReGina Crawford

Quintana. Not sure what the look on her face is telling him, he leans back in his chair and folds his arms across his chest waiting on her to speak to him. She doesn't say a word. She just stands there staring at him for the longest time. Then out of the blue, she reaches her hand out to him. He places his hand in hers, and she closes her eyes as she lets out the breath she was holding. He stands, and she turns and walks towards her office still holding his hand.

Once inside her office, she closes and locks the door. She turns back to him, and wraps her arms around him. Before he knows it, Quintana is crying in earnest against his chest. He is both shocked and surprised, but simply wraps his arms tighter around her whispering *'Sshh'* in her ear. They continue to stand that way for over fifteen minutes before her crying begins to subside. At which point Quentin lifts her face to his, and kisses her wholeheartedly on the lips. He doesn't stop kissing her until the need to breathe becomes paramount, and then he only stops kissing her long enough to draw two very needed gulps of air into his lungs.

Once he is satisfied that she has been thoroughly kissed, he looks her in the eyes and asks, "What was all the crying about?"

"I never . . . thought . . . that I . . . would see you . . . again," she replies as she tries to catch her breath.

"Why would you think that sweetheart," he asks thoroughly confused.

"Because . . . I haven't . . . seen or heard . . . from you . . . in two weeks," she states still trying to catch her breath.

Noticing that she is really struggling to catch her breath, Quentin walks her over to the couch in her office and sits down placing her on his lap. Which is really awkward due to the state of his arousal, but he doesn't let her up. "Sweetheart, I'm not going anywhere. You said you needed time to think, and I was giving it to you. I

Food From The Heart

came by today because you were taking too long to call me, and I couldn't go another day without seeing you, tasting you."

Quintana starts crying again, much to Quentin's surprise. He gives her a few minutes to get these new set of tears out of her system before raising her face to his once again. "Why are you crying now," he asks.

"Because I've fallen in love with you, and I wasn't supposed to," she states breathlessly.

"Why weren't you supposed to fall in love with me," he asks around a smile.

"I just wasn't, that's all," she responds.

"Well, I for one am glad that you fell in love with me, because I've fallen in love with you too," he replies. Quintana starts crying again, and Quentin is at a loss as to what to do. "More tears, I wasn't expecting this," he whispers.

"They are tears of joy and relief," she states, "I never thought that I would get to hear those words from your lips."

"Well you've heard them and they are true," he responds, "I love you sweetheart. More than life itself, and I couldn't stand to be away from you a minute longer."

This time Quintana kisses him, and his erection gets harder than it's ever been. She feels it moving against her backside as it struggles for room to expand, and she grinds her hips against it. Quentin hisses air through his teeth at her movements, and that only encourages her to move a little more.

He grabs her hips with both hands in an attempt to keep her from moving, "You've got to stop that or I'm going to embarrass myself," he whispers.

"It seems somebody is in desperate need of relief," she states while trying not to laugh.

Quentin notices how hard she is struggling not to laugh, "Oh, so you think this is funny do you?" At her nod, "We'll see how funny it is when I get you home tonight," he quips around his own laughter.

"I can't wait," replies Quintana.

"You say that now, but know this – there will be no calling Uncle later tonight. I have two weeks to make up for," he states with a look on his face that let's Quintana know that he is deadly serious.

"Just you remember you said that later on. Your place or mine?"

"Mine," states Quentin firmly.
"Then I'll let you get back to your menu, and I'll see you later tonight." Quintana and Quentin stand at the same time, and she looks him up and down. "You might want to do something with that before you step out of here," she states while looking pointedly at his erection.

"There is only one thing that's going to make that go away, and unfortunately I can't get it right now." Quintana lowers her lashes to hide her embarrassment. "I know you are not trying to play shy now," he quips around a smile.

"No, I'm not playing shy," she states as she lifts her lashes, "I just didn't want you to see how much I want to give IT to you right here, right now."

It's Quentin's turn to close his eyes as desire stronger than any he has ever felt overtakes his mind, body, and soul. "Out! Now," he states without even opening his eyes. When he doesn't hear her

Food From The Heart

moving, he states, "I mean it, or this whole restaurant will hear us both shouting to the stars."

Quintana giggles as she makes her way to the door. Once Quentin hears the door open and close, he sits back down on the couch and places his head in his hands as he desperately tries to calm down his over aroused body. After about ten minutes, he feels calm enough to go back to his table. He orders and eats his dinner before leaving the restaurant to get ready for Quintana's arrival later that night.

ReGina Crawford

Gluttony

When Quintana arrives at Quentin's place around midnight, she can't believe her eyes. He has transformed his place into a desert oasis complete with a shimmering pool of water and sand – SAND. "Oh my," she states, "I wasn't expecting this."

"You should know by now to expect the unexpected when dealing with me," is his response.

That's when Quintana notices how he's dressed – Desert Sheik. "Damn," is all she can form her mouth to say until she notices how aroused he is, "Aww Shit," is what comes out of her mouth next.

Following her line of sight, Quentin smiles before saying, "Aww Shit is right, sweetheart. I told you you have two weeks to make up for, and I plan to get it all tonight. Your bath is ready, and I'll be waiting."

Quintana is praying for a miracle as she makes her way to her bath, or at least for an extra dose of stamina for she knows tonight is going to be a long, hard night.

After her bath, Quintana dons the harem outfit she finds waiting for her in the bathroom. It is nothing but a few panels of completely sheer fabric with no ties, buttons, or any other type of fasteners. As she walks the panels swirl around her giving away teasing glimpses

Food From The Heart

of her flesh with every step. As she hits the top of the steps, Quentin looks up and sees her. His eyes become glued to every inch of her body as she slowly makes her way down the stairs. The teasing glimpses of her naked flesh cause his body to become more and more aroused, and he knows she is taking her time walking to him just to prolong the teasing of his senses.

When she is finally standing in front of him, he stares into her eyes with his hands clenched into fists at his side as he tries to convey to her what she is in store for tonight. Understanding every word that his eyes are saying, she nods her head to indicate she is ready for all that he has in mind. "Are you sure," he asks barely above a whisper. At her nod, he takes a deep breath before saying, "As beautiful as this is, it has to go." Then he rips it from her body just as his mouth latches on her breasts, and he suckles as though he is starving. The sensations are too much for Quintana, and she lets her head fall back as a ragged moan escapes her lips. Quentin then runs his tongue between her breasts down to the heart of her, and begins feasting on her as though he hasn't eaten in weeks. Quintana climaxes instantly, but that doesn't stop him from getting his fill. Even as he feels her legs getting weak he doesn't remove his mouth, he simply eases her down to the pillows on the floor. Four climaxes later, Quentin looks up into her glowing face and smiles. "Thought you said you were ready," he asks.

"I did too," is her breathless response. "It seems no matter how ready I think I am, you always manage to drain everything from me."

"Baby, I haven't even gotten started yet," he quips as he lowers his head to her stomach.

She grabs his head as she states, "I knew you were going to say that." Knowing that there is nothing she can do to stop the assault of his lips, tongue, hands, and body, Quintana just lays back and enjoys the skill of the man she loves.

ReGina Crawford

Quentin brings her to two more climaxes with his mouth and hands before placing his body over hers. He starts out slow savoring every movement of his body entering into hers, but when she wraps her arms and legs around him he instantly increases the pace. Her moans quickly escalate to screams of ecstasy as she climaxes twice as a result of the deep hard thrusts he's giving her. He then slows the pace back down not wanting the night to be over, and knowing that if keeps up his current pace it would be all over for him. The slow grind he initiates is even more detrimental to her senses than the fast pace he just subjected her to, and she finds herself caught up in an orgasm so overwhelming that her whole body is shaking from the force of it.

Still keeping the pace slow and easy Quentin whispers in her ear, "This is the last one for this round." Quintana whimpers at the thought of experiencing another orgasm. "I haven't nearly made up for the two weeks I had to go through without you baby, so it's going to be a long night. But I do promise to take care of you all night long, in every way." He then grabs her hips to bring her closer to him, and the pace slowly increases until he is giving her deep penetrating thrusts again. It isn't long before his orgasm begins to over take him. "Now baby! Come with me," he shouts just as his orgasm takes over his body.

"Quentin," shouts Quintana as she climaxes with him.

"Quintana," shouts Quentin as his orgasm shakes his entire body. Once he is spent and they fall to the pillows together, he looks her in the eyes and whispers, "I love you."

Quintana's eyes quickly mist at his admission, but she quickly whispers back, "I love you too."

The kiss that he bestows upon her springs forth the tears of joy in her eyes, and he kisses them away. "Sleep," he whispers, "I'll be waking you up in a couple of hours for round two." When her eyes

Food From The Heart

widen, he smiles before saying, "Yes, there will be a round two, and maybe a round three if I don't get enough in round two. So sleep while you can."

Quintana takes advantage of the catnap he's giving her, since she knows that he is true to his word about the other two rounds. Just before she falls asleep she thinks to herself, *'God, I love this man, and I have truly missed this.'* She falls asleep with a smile on her face.

Quentin too falls asleep with a smile on his face, but true to his word he is waking her up two hours later to start round two. Round two is so close to round one in intensity, that round three is out of the question for tonight but there's always tomorrow thinks Quentin as he falls asleep.

ReGina Crawford

Brunch

It's almost noon by the time Quentin and Quintana wake up the next day, but both are still smiling from last night's activities. "Good Morning," they both say at the same time before falling into a fit of laughter. Quentin grabs her around the waist before throwing a leg over her to hold her in place for his good morning kiss, which quickly escalates into a kiss of passion. Before she knows it, Quentin throws her legs over his shoulders and begins making love to her with his mouth. It doesn't take her long to reach an orgasm which he ignores as he continues his afternoon feast.

"I love your taste," he whispers in her ear after her third orgasm just as he enters her warm center. He makes love to her as though he has had to do without her for far too long. As he feels her body begin to spasm with her next orgasm, he whispers in her ear, "That's it baby. Let it go. Come for me."
She follows his dictate as though she is under some sort of spell, and climaxes while screaming his name. Once she's able to speak again, she whispers in his ear, "Your turn to come for me." Then she grips her legs tighter around his waist as she moves her hips against him. She hears him suck in his breath at her movements, "That's it, let go. Come for me baby. Let me feel it."

Her words send him over the edge, and he lets go screaming her name through his orgasm. "Damn, I wasn't ready to come yet," he

Food From The Heart

states once he has regained control of his breathing. "You did that on purpose," he states while looking into her eyes.

"Yes I did," she replies. "I don't think it's fair that you are the only one who's been engaging in oral feasts. So, now it's my turn," she states as she flips him over and makes her way down his chest and stomach to his already thickening manhood. She glides her tongue from his tip to his base before caressing his testicles with her tongue and lips. His moans of pleasure encourage her to continue to make love to him this way, however, before she can make him climax, he flips her back over and enters her just as he goes over the edge. "That's not fair," she pouts as he continues to stroke her hard and deep. But the rest of her words are cut off as she is suddenly hit with an orgasm of her own, and much to Quentin's surprise he experiences another orgasm of his own.

"Damn Baby, what are you doing to me," asks Quentin when he has regained control of his breathing.

"The question is, what are you doing to me," replies Quintana. "I have experienced more orgasms with you than I thought possible. And it seems no matter how tired I am, the moment you look at me, touch me, I become putty in your hands."

"And you don't think that you have the same effect on me? Baby, all I have to do is smell your scent, and I'm a goner. Just like right now, I can smell your aroused scent and I'm rock hard." Quintana drops her eyes at his words, and he puts his hand under her chin until she looks back at him. "Too late to be embarrassed now, sweetheart. Besides you know what you do to me, and I want you to know that I love you and everything that you do to me."

"I love you too," responds Quintana. They lie back on the pillows and enjoy being in one another's arms basking in the afterglow of their love making. Sometime later, Quentin's stomach growls loudly indicating that he is hungry. "Guess it's time to feed you something other than me," she quips around a smile.

"But I love having you as breakfast, lunch, dinner, late night snack, and every other type of dining there is," he replies while trying to hold back his laughter at the look on her face. "It's true, shall I prove it?"
Quintana quickly scrambles off of the pillows before replying, "No, I think you've proven it enough times. But you need to eat something substantial to keep up your strength for all of your other dining pleasures." She squeals while running towards the bathroom as Quentin makes a move to get off of the pillows.

Quentin leans back against the pillows, since he knows that if he joins her in the bathroom, he'll be making love to her again. He's too weak to do that properly without getting some real food in his system. So, while she's taking a shower, he heads to the kitchen to cook them something to eat. Just as he is placing her omelet on a plate, she emerges from the bedroom. "Your breakfast awaits," he states.

Quintana licks her lips while smiling at him before asking, "I'm a little confused, what's on the menu? The omelet or you?"

Quentin arches an eyebrow while pondering her question, and then he looks down and notices his state of undress and his growing manhood. He then looks her in the eyes and asks, "Which do you prefer?"

"They're both very tempting but since I know that I won't be able to stop you when you get started, I'll start with the omelet."

Quentin starts laughing, and hands her the plate with the omelet. While she enjoys her breakfast, he cooks his own. When her plate is empty and she is sitting across from him with a satisfied smile on her face, he asks, "Are you ready for the second part of your meal?"

"And that would be?"

Food From The Heart

"Me of course," quips Quentin around a smile.

"After a shower, you're on."

"Hmm, a shower huh? I like the sound of that."

"I've already had my shower," she responds trying to hide her smile.

"But I need you wash my back."

"Just how much showering is going to go on if I'm in there with you?"

"I plan to do a whole lot of showering. Showering kisses from your neck to your feet, and especially between your legs."

"See, that's exactly why I wasn't planning on showering with you."

"But you will enjoy the hell out of the experience. I promise you."

Quintana closes her eyes at the visual image his words bring to mind, and Quentin takes that as an invitation. So, he picks her up and carries her into the shower and makes good on his words.

ReGina Crawford

Double Dealing

Quentin and Quintana's relationship is back on track, and she has since moved back into her home although she spends more time at Quentin's place than her own house. The contracts are drafted and signed, and construction begins on the business complex. Although Sylvia has been active behind the scenes, she has kept a low profile on the streets. Dirt Doctor and Jackal have not been able to find out where her funding is coming from or who she has working with her. The only good news Quentin has had in the last few weeks is that if Charles Givens is Mr. Red, he can't change his appearance since this is a long term deal.

One night Quentin decides to take a walk around the construction site before heading home, and notices some familiar cars parked near the construction trucks. Not wanting to bring attention to himself, he crouches down low and moves closer to see what his business partner is up to. Once he gets closer, he hears some familiar and unfamiliar voices engaged in a heated discussion.

"Sir it's impossible to get a shipment moved on these trucks. McNair's employment process is so tight that we can't even get any of our men employed on this project. Hell we can't even get near the site without being questioned."

"We're here tonight aren't we," asks a familiar voice.

Food From The Heart

"Well yes, and I'm still waiting on the security guard to walk up on us at any moment."

"I've taken care of him for the moment. He'll be out for another hour or so. Now we need to formulate a plan to get someone from the organization on this construction crew. Who do we have that doesn't have a criminal record and has some construction experience," asks the voice that Quentin knows belongs to Charles Givens.

"No one, but my wife's younger brother is returning home after graduating from college and he needs a job. He is an architect, but he's such a goody-goody that I don't know if we could get him to do what we want."

"Then it will be up to you to convince him to do what we want. Make it a condition of him gaining employment," states the familiar voice. "We need to get things moving or we are going to lose a lot of money, not to mention that my reputation is on the line. Also, I hear that Ms Sylvia is back up to her old tricks, and might be getting closer to trying to take a bite out of my ass again. I want to get this done so I can get out of this hell hole, and back to a more moderate climate. Plus McNair is so damn sweet he's making my teeth hurt. I was so hoping he was one we could convert into the organization, but I don't see that happening."

"I'll get on it right away boss," states the underling with the brother-in-law in need of employment.

The group breaks up and heads to their cars, and Quentin makes sure he is not detected. He is so glad he did not park his car anywhere near the site, and as he walks back the way he came he makes a mental note to hire this brother-in-law so he can close this case.

Once he arrives back home, he takes a quick shower and cleans his shoes and suit from the construction grime he picked up while listening to Givens and his crew. After getting cleaned up, he receives a phone call from the guard at the site telling him that he received a visit from Mr. Givens and that he believes he was slipped some type of drug that put him out. Quentin informs him to bag up anything that he ate, drank, or touched, and that he would deal with it in the morning.

The next morning, Quentin arrives at the site bright and early to collect the items from the guard, and assures him that there is nothing to worry about before sending him home. Quentin takes the items back to his office to send them off to be analyzed, and to inform the Dirt Doctor and the Jackal of the latest developments. He also makes arrangements to have each of the construction vehicles and the site outfitted with surveillance equipment so that he can capture any future clandestine meetings held by Mr. Givens.

When a new architect applies for a position with the project, Quentin interviews him for the position hoping it's the man he's been waiting on. After the interview, Quentin sends his information, pictures, and the prints and DNA he retrieved from his water glass off to the Dirt Doctor and the Jackal just to verify that the gentleman is who he thinks he is. Once his identity is confirmed to be the brother-in-law in question, Quentin makes him a job offer that is too good to be true. Quentin figures he'll wait until Marquise Redmon has received a few nice pay checks before he tries to bring him in on his "undercover" dealings.

Once Quentin sees that Marquise is enjoying his pay, he pulls him to the side to set his plan in motion. They're in Quentin's office going over the plans for the rest of Quentin's offices at the new complex. "Marquise, how would you like to add a few thousand dollars to your pocket," asks Quentin.

Marquise looks up from the blueprints with one eyebrow raised, and questions in his eyes. "Huh," he asks.

Food From The Heart

"Look we've been working together for a few weeks now, and I feel like I can trust you."

"Sure boss, you can trust me."

"Great! I need to alter the plans for my office, but I need the changes to stay between just us. The regular crew will not be constructing these plans. I have a special crew for that, okay?"

"Okay. What do you have in mind," asks Marquise curious as ever to find out what the "straight-laced" Quentin's plans are for his office.

"I need a small room built inside my offices that will be concealed from anyone entering my offices. The entrance to this room will be through my private bathroom, but the entrance can't look like an entrance. Feel me?"

"Sure boss, I feel you."

Quentin and Marquise spend the next half hour designing the secret room and its entrance before Marquise goes back to work on the regular plans for the complex. However, once he gets off work, he wastes no time telling his brother-in-law about the plans that Quentin has for this secret room. Of course, Charles Givens' lackey quickly rushes over to tell his boss about these plans.

"It seems McNair may not be as goody-goody as he appears to be boss."

"Hmm, you may be right. I wonder what this secret room is for. He could just be a cheat, and the room is for all his extra-curricular activities since I find it hard to believe he could be up to anything illegal. I just don't think he has the stomach for it, but I could be wrong. We'll just have to keep a close watch on his movements."

The Move

Construction on the complex is seventy-five percent complete, and Mr. Givens and his associates are unaware that Quentin knows all about the secret room and passageway that they had Marquise construct under their offices.

Quentin has been aware of all of the dealings of his business partners as a result of having installed surveillance equipment throughout the complex and construction vehicles, and knows that they are close to making a major move. He has put his superiors on notice to have a team ready to go at a moment's notice since he knows that they are going to try to move as quickly and quietly as possible. Charles Givens appears to be extremely anxious to get his deal complete, and get the hell out Dallas.

One Saturday night Quentin, Keith, Kyle, and Kendrick are in his secret room checking the surveillance footage from the day before, when they see movement on one of the digital screens. Zooming in, they notice that it's Charles Givens and his crew. He is unloading large crates from a truck that closely resembles one of the construction trucks for the complex, and a zoom on the plate confirms that it is indeed one of the trucks from the site. Quentin quickly jots down the plate number so that he can retrieve the images from the digital camera located in the lights and axels of the truck. They watch as the crew continues to unload the truck and take the crates into the passageways that lead to Charles' secret room, and there are quite a few.

Once they have unloaded the truck, Charles and his crew leave the site. Quentin and his crew make their way over to the room to inspect the crates.

"Just as I suspected," states Quentin, "they're filled with guns."

"It seems your Mr. Givens is indeed the illegal arms runner that Sylvia thinks he is," remarks Kyle.

"The question is, how are you going to bring him down and not piss the lady off," quips Keith. When the others turn and look at him, he adds, "She already doesn't like or trust you, and if you take away her life's work I don't think she's going to take it well."
Quentin concedes, "I know you're right. Which creates the question of how do I let her bring them down without her knowing I had anything to do with it."

"You would let her take credit for bringing them down," asks Kendrick.

"I'm willing to let her think that she brought them down. My superiors would know the truth, and I'm hoping that it will also help me locate the traitor in my camp," responds Quentin.

"As though the situation isn't complicated enough already, the kid wants to throw another wrinkle in the mix," Kyle states to Keith as though Quentin isn't standing there.

"I'm not throwing another wrinkle in the mix," responds Quentin, "I've already formulated a plan to get Sylvia involved." At their *have-you-lost-your-mind* look, Quentin states, "Trust me fellas, this will work."

"Let's get out of here before someone comes back," states Keith and the rest of them agree.

Once they are back in Quentin's office, he informs them of his plan. All four agree that the plan just might work, but that they would have to keep tight tabs on Ms Williams to make sure that things didn't get out of hand.

Later that night, Quentin lets the Dirt Doctor and the Jackal know what he's found in the secret room created by Charles Givens, and about his plan to use Ms Williams to bring them down. In order to assure that they are brought to justice and not disposed of by Ms Williams, they will need to step up their surveillance of her without being detected. They also need to make sure that the traitor in Quentin's camp does not get word on what is going down, so the decision is made not to let Brad know what is going on.

Two days later, the Dirt Doctor and the Jackal let Quentin know that they have the necessary surveillance in place, so he can put his plan involving Sylvia in place. Now all Quentin has to do is find her since he hasn't seen her in quite some time. *'Maybe I should let her find me by driving through the parts of town that she thinks I shouldn't visit,'* Quentin thinks to himself.

The next day, Quentin makes like he is scouting more land and buildings in an area of town known to be controlled by Charles Givens' organization. *'Here's hoping Sylvia is still on the prowl looking for her arms dealer,'* he thinks as he's driving. Quentin has been driving the neighborhood for more than an hour, and is just about ready to give up when he spots Ms Williams three cars behind him. *'It's about time you showed up,'* is his thought upon seeing her. He pulls over after driving a few more blocks, pretending he's interested in a recently vacated building.

Food From The Heart

He's not out of the car five minutes before Sylvia walks up to him. "Scouting property for your next project already," she asks sarcastically.

Quentin spins around as though he is surprised to hear her voice, "Where did you come from," he asks.

"Since you're back to cruising my neighborhood and already doing business with the shaky Mr. Givens, yes I am following you."

"What is it you don't like about Mr. Givens?"

"He's as dirty as they come, and if you're not careful, you're going to get buried beneath his dirt."

"Why do you think he's dirty?"

"I don't think that he's dirty, I know that he's dirty. I just need to prove it, but he's as slippery as he is dirty."

"I've seen no evidence of him being dirty, but there is . . .," begins Quentin, "No I don't think he has anything to do with that."

"To do with what? What are you talking about," asks an animated Sylvia.

"It's probably nothing," states Quentin.
"Just spit it out," counters Sylvia.

"Well my night security guard thinks that he's been slipped something to put him out for a few hours a couple of times, and he says he always feels that way after a visit from Mr. Givens. But we have found no evidence of anything strange going on after he feels that way."

ReGina Crawford

"That's exactly what I'm talking about, dirty and slippery," comments Sylvia. "I'm telling you now, you are going to wind up on the wrong side of the law dealing with that man."

"If he is doing something illegal, I'm not involved so I have nothing to worry about," states Quentin indignantly. "Besides there is no evidence that he's doing anything. He tells the guard that he just likes to make sure that his investment in the project is well guarded. They talk a little sports, and then he's gone. They only thing he's ever done is shake the man's hand, so how could he have slipped him something?"

"It was on his hand," states Sylvia out loud.

"How is that possible? Wouldn't he have been affected by it as well if it was on his hand?"

"Not if he took something to counter act the drug before applying it to his hand," responds Sylvia.
"How can I prove that's what happened? And how can I find out what he's up to? I don't want to be caught up in any illegal dealings," states Quentin.

"Would you like my help Mr. McNair?"

'I knew you would not be able to resist the bait Ms Williams,' Quentin thinks to himself. "How can you help," he asks.

"You may not want to get too involved with this, so I don't think I'll tell you want my plans are. I just need some information from you." Sylvia then proceeds to shoot a dozen or so questions at him about the project and Charles Givens involvement in it.

After Quentin has answered all of her questions, Sylvia gets back in her car and drives away. Quentin continues to scope out the

Food From The Heart

building just in case anyone saw the two of them talking, and wanted to make it look like they were working together.

Clandestine Affairs

When Quentin comes from the back of the building, one of Charles' henchmen is waiting by his car. "Hey Jason, what's good man," asks Quentin smiling.

"Ain't nothing good when it comes to Sylvia Williams. What were the two of you talking about?"

"You know that crazy lady too," asks Quentin. "That woman has been dogging me since I first arrived in this city, asking me questions like she has a right to be all up in my business. And she doesn't like being told that something is none of her business."

"Yeah, that's Sylvia. Once she sinks her teeth into something or someone, it's hard to get her to back off."
"Then how do you get rid of her," asks Quentin.

"You don't," states Jason.

"What do you mean you don't? I don't plan to spend the rest of my days telling that lady to get out of business, and I'm tired of her just popping up out of the blue."

"She's been dogging us for some years now and even though she may lay low from time to time, she never goes away."

Food From The Heart

"Damn, that's the last thing I wanted to hear," states Quentin as he looks at his watch. "Oh shit," he states, "I'm going to be late for lunch with my lady, man. I've got to go." As he opens the door to his car, he calls over his shoulder, "See you later."

As Quentin drives away, Jason gets on his phone to let his boss know about seeing Sylvia talking to Quentin. "Yeah boss, I think we need to move up our time table as well. See you at the office in thirty." Jason hangs up and makes his way to his car unaware that Sylvia is watching him.

Quentin arrives at the restaurant without a minute to spare, and is immediately seated at what has been dubbed "his table". Quintana exits the kitchen just as he opens his menu which he quickly lowers as he graces her with his most charming smile. "Good Afternoon," he greets her.

"Good Afternoon to you as well. I thought I was going to be stood up," she responds.

"Not on your life. I just ran into a little snag on my way here, but I was coming."

Ignoring the double meaning of his last statement, Quintana asks, "Nothing serious I hope."

"Nothing serious, and actually it was kind of expected. So I was able to take care of it fairly quickly." Changing the subject before she can ask too many questions, Quentin asks, "So what's on the menu for today?"

"All depends on what you have an appetite for," quips Quintana.

"Are you sure you want to go there? You know I always have an appetite for you, which you would see evidence of if you would look under the table cloth."

ReGina Crawford

Quintana closes her eyes at the thoughts that run through her mind. "I should have known not to get you started," she states.

"Yes you should have. Now what am I having for lunch?"

"I've prepared you a seafood dish I'm thinking about adding to the menu. It will be out shortly," she states as she heads back into the kitchen.

In the meantime, Jason meets Charles at their offices away from the project site. "Hey Boss," greets Jason. "It looks like Ms Williams is crawling back out of her hole, and is planning to harass Mr. McNair. Apparently today is not his first run in with her, and he asked me how to get her to stop dogging him. When I told him you can't, he didn't seem too happy about it."

"Which makes me think that Mr. McNair isn't as squeaky clean as he appears. If he didn't have anything to hide, he wouldn't be so concerned about her being in his business. Maybe we can kill two birds with one stone," Charles thinks out loud.

"How so Boss?"

"We can make Mr. McNair look like he's the illegal arms runner which would get Ms Williams off our asses, and we can let her uncover what illegal activities he really has going on. This way, if he doesn't get busted, we could possibly get in on his business dealings in the future."

"Great idea Boss. So are we just going to lay back and see what develops between Williams and McNair?"

"Yes, I think that's best for now."

Once Quentin finishes his lunch with Quintana, he heads back to his real estate office to let the Dirt Doctor and the Jackal know that he

Food From The Heart

has made contact with Sylvia, and raised her curiosity about Charles and his crew. He also lets Keith, Kyle, and Kendrick in on the latest developments with his "little project".

After following Jason to Charles Given's office, Sylvia heads over to the development that Quentin is building to plan how she is going to sneak in later that night. She needs to get a full layout of the project in the daylight before she makes her foray on to the project at night. She notices the normal security camera setup, the guard station, the entrances and exits for the construction crews, as well as, the entrance she assumes is used by McNair and Givens. After getting the 'lay of the land', she hacks into the security firm being used by McNair to find out who will be on duty tonight so she knows who she's dealing with in the event she runs into the guard later tonight. Once she finalizes her plans for the evening, she sits back and waits for nightfall.

*****

At precisely midnight, Sylvia enters the construction site unaware that Quentin, Keith, Kyle, and Kendrick are watching her on the surveillance cameras. Having been at other sites used by Givens, it doesn't take her long to find Givens' secret room and take snapshots of his gun shipment before breaking into his file cabinets to find out who the guns are meant for. Unfortunately, she isn't able to find the information she's looking for, so she adds her own "party favor" to the crates.

Quentin is surprised to see that she is using the same thread thin surveillance equipment that he uses to monitor Charles' secret room. He makes a mental note to get in touch with Dirt Doctor about the results of the Heat Seek operation. Noticing the slight change in Quentin's demeanor K cubed, as Quentin calls them, fold their arms across their chest waiting on an explanation. Seeing the movement out of the corner of his eye, Quentin turns to face them with a *what-the-hell-is-wrong-with-you* look on his face.

ReGina Crawford

"We know you saw something, what was it," asks Kyle.

"I have no idea what you're talking about," responds Quentin.

"Yes you do. We've been around you enough to know when something doesn't sit well with you, and you saw something on camera that didn't sit well with you. And unless you want us to beat it out of you, then you will tell us," comes back Keith, the Dirty Harry of the crew.
"I'm tired of you making idol threats. Why don't we just find out who can beat who," responds Quentin.

The peace keeper Kendrick steps between the two before things can get out of hand, "Now children, play nice," he quips while looking back and forth between the two.

"Alright," states Quentin not really wanting to waste time whooping Keith's ass at the moment. "I received word that there might be some double dealing in my camp, and the fact that Sylvia is using the same surveillance equipment I'm using lets me know that it's someone high up in my camp and who their double dealing with."

"Damn," state K cubed at once.

"Why does everything have to sound like surround sound when the three of you are together?"

"Don't be a smart-ass", all three speak at once again.

"See there it goes again," states Quentin. When they give him their *I'm-going-to-kick-your-ass* look, Quentin puts his hands in the air in mock surrender. "Look fellas, I would love to stay and play with you, but I have work to do before the sun comes up. So, let's get out of here, and I'll talk to you later." The men close up shop, and head out.

Food From The Heart

Turning Up the Heat

While the other three head home, Quentin heads to his real estate office to talk to the Dirt Doctor. Once inside his secret room, he places the call to get the results of the Heat Seek operation. "Black Mambo. Lockjaw in place," he states when the line is answered.

"Dirt Doctor. Secure."

"Details. Sylvia Williams has the same surveillance equipment I'm using. Need Heat Seek update."

"Heat Seek results not conclusive. The person you are seeking is high on the ladder, but is not working on the side of evil. They are seeking justice. Most likely the person who is helping Ms Williams. Still be careful."

As the line goes dead, Quentin is left pondering who in his organization is helping Sylvia and why. Deciding not to wait on the outcome of this operation, Quentin decides to do some more research on Sylvia's team to see if someone close to them is a part of the organization, and seeking justice.

After three hours of searching, Quentin thinks he's found something in pictures from an award ceremony for Sylvia's team years ago. However, it appears that some of the pictures from the roll are missing, and they would allow to him to put the pieces of the puzzle together. He makes a call to the Jackal. "Lion Hunter," states Quentin when the line is picked up on the other end.

Jackal."

"Details. Negatives from medal ceremony for Williams' team after the mission in Africa. Heat Seek evidence."

"Peace Time minus twelve."

The line goes dead, and Quentin looks at his watch. It's just after o-six hundred. He might as well take a shower while he waits. At exactly seven twenty-eight he receives the complete roll of pictures. "Damn, who would have thought she was involved. How is she getting materials to Sylvia without getting detected," he asks out loud. "It's time to wrap this case up, and get some answers. But how do I get Sylvia to rush her move?"

Needing to think, Quentin heads home to work out. After forty-five minutes on the weight bench and treadmill, an idea comes to him. He makes a few calls to put his plan in motion. Once he has brought Kyle and Keith up to date on his plans, he takes a much need nap since the rest of the day and tomorrow are going to be long ones.

*****

The next day at exactly three o'clock, Kyle, Keith, and few other police officers show up at the construction site demanding to speak with the person or persons in charge. Quentin and Charles make their way to the guard shack after being summoned by the guard on duty.

"Is there something we can do for you officers," asks Quentin.

Food From The Heart

"Yes there is," answers Keith. "We have been receiving reports of activity taking place at this site after the normal crew has left for the day, and we would like to take a look around."

"Just one minute son," states Charles, "we haven't done anything to warrant you being here."

"Do you have something to hide sir," asks Keith.

"No, I don't have anything to hide, but this is sounding like harassment. We are upstanding business men trying to bring jobs to a poverty stricken area, and you're here because of reports of activity after hours. That sounds like bullshit to me."

Kyle walks up on Charles until they are nose-to-nose before speaking, "It sounds to me like you have something to hide. What's your name and what's your involvement with this project?"

"I'm Charles Givens, and I'm a large investor in this project," answers Charles not looking the least bit intimidated. "What's your name and rank?"

"Well Mr. Givens, I'm Lieutenant Wright and this was just going to be a routine inquiry. But since you seem to have a problem with us being here, I think my men will be doing a thorough investigation of the site."

"Hold on a minute," steps in Quentin, "I'm Quentin McNair and I'm in charge of this project," he states when all eyes turn his way. "How about everyone cool their tempers, and step into my office to see if we can straighten this out?"

"I would love to go to your office, lead the way," responds Kyle. Then to his men, he says, "Keith, you, Tom, and Jim come with me. The rest of you post up here and keep your eyes sharp."

The officers and Charles follow Quentin to his offices on the construction site. Once inside, Quentin leans against his desk as the officers post up around the room, and Charles takes a seat in one of the chairs in front of Quentin's desk.

"Now officers, I believe we can resolve any misunderstandings in a civilized manner," begins Quentin. "Can we start at the beginning? What exactly brought you to our development this afternoon?"

"Our office has received a number of phone calls about trucks entering the site and unloading crates late at night for the past week, and the chief sent us out here to investigate since some of the calls came directly to him," answers Kyle. "We've done some background checking on you Mr. McNair and your company, and found nothing out of the ordinary. However, your investor Mr. Givens has a few red flags attached to his name, and thus the reason why we are here."

"What do you mean red flags," asks Quentin and Charles at the same time.

Deciding to ignore Charles, Kyle continues to address Quentin, "It seems Mr. Givens has been investigated in the past for everything from gun running to drug running."

"None of those allegations were ever proven," huffs Charles, "and I resent you bringing them up to my new business partner. Those rumors were started by businessmen who were pissed because I was awarded contracts they were after and didn't get," he continues with his voice reaching a near shout. "They were nothing but a bunch of sore losers."

"Let's remain calm here Charles. My company didn't find anything out of the ordinary in your business dealings, so that is the reason we made the deal with you. So you don't have to worry about our contract being nullified by this small mishap," Quentin states to

Food From The Heart

Charles. Seeing Charles visibly relax, Quentin turns back to Kyle, "Lieutenant Wright, I appreciate you having to do your investigation as a result of the phone calls, and I welcome you and your men to take a thorough look around. I don't think that you will find anything out of the ordinary since the site is equipped with surveillance equipment, and my security firm would have alerted me to any unusual activity at that the site."

"You have surveillance cameras on the site," asks Kyle and Charles at the same time.

"Of course," states Quentin while addressing Charles, "you would be surprised how many times construction sites are ripped off by their competitors. They stock pile stolen supplies to try to be the lowest bidder on projects their bidding on." He then turns to Kyle, "If you would like to see the footage from any night in question, I could get you the disks."

"I would appreciate that Mr. McNair, and your cooperation with this investigation will be noted," responds Kyle.

"I'll call the security office, and have the disks sent over to you right away." Quentin then moves to his phone to make the call.

While he's on the phone, Kyle addresses Charles, "You could learn a lesson or two from your partner over there. The best way to squash suspicion is to be cooperative not antagonistic."

"The disks should be delivered within the half hour," states Quentin after hanging up the phone.

"Thanks again Mr. McNair," responds Kyle. "We'll take our leave now, and get back to you if we have any more questions," he continues addressing Quentin. He then turns to Charles, "You fellas have a good day now," he states sarcastically.

Boiling Point

Once the officers leave the office, Quentin turns to Charles and states with venom in his voice, "In the future, it would be in your best interest to keep a level head with the authorities."

"Wait just a damn minute here," begins Charles pissed for being reprimanded like a misbehaved child.

"No," quietly shouts Quentin, "you wait a damn minute. I will not have any type of law enforcement snooping around my development for any reason." As Charles gets to his feet, Quentin walks up to him until they are nose-to-nose, "I suggest you take care and not give them any reason to come back." He then turns, walks back to his desk, takes his seat, and picks up the phone, dismissing Charles with no uncertainty.

Never having experienced this side of Quentin, Charles is unsure of how to deal with him, and decides to head to his own offices so that he can get his business taken care of and get the hell out of dodge. However, as he plays the events of the afternoon over in his mind, his temperature rises higher than it was when the officers were present. "That little son of bitch has another thing coming if he thinks he can just dismiss me like I'm insignificant," huffs Charles as he enters his office. "Just wait till my business is concluded, I'm going to break his fucking neck."

Food From The Heart

"Boss, what the hell is going on," asks an anxious Jason.

"That muther fucker had the nerve to talk down to me," states Charles at a near yell. "I plan to teach that yung'un a lesson when we're done here."

"Slow down. Are you talking about one of the police officers," asks Jason.

"McNair! I'm talking about McNair!"

"What could McNair tell the police? He doesn't know anything."

"He didn't tell the police anything! But he had the nerve to check me then dismiss me from his office!"

"Boss, calm down. Can you start at the beginning?"
"McNair handled the police like a pro, which makes me think he's not as squeaky clean as we first thought. Did you know that he has surveillance cameras set up on the site?"

"What? Cameras? Where are they?"

"I have no idea, but if he's got any of our after hour activities on tape he's just sent them to the police," states Givens as he takes a seat behind his desk after making himself a drink. "But that's not what's got me pissed. After he got rid of the police, he had the nerve to tell me to handle my business better so that the police don't have a reason to come back. Then he just sat at his desk, and proceeded to ignore me while he made a phone call."

"Are you fucking serious?"

"Yes, I'm serious! I'm also serious about breaking his fucking neck with my bare hands!" Charles takes a drink from his glass before taking a deep breath to calm himself down, so that he can handle the business at hand. "But that's going to have to wait. We need to take care of our deal before the police have a chance to completely analyze those tapes."

Charles calls in his crew, and they get their business in order so that their deal can go down tonight.

*****

Quentin calls Kyle to let him know that the plan is a go based on the way Givens walked out of his office. Quentin can't help but laugh as he recalls the look on Charles's face as he stood toe-to-toe with him, and gave him the business. "I definitely threw him for loop with that move. He's never seen me as a hard case. As a matter of fact, I would be willing to bet he thought I was a 3-ply."

Kyle is laughing on the other end as Quentin relays the events that took place after he and his team left. "3-ply? What the hell is that," asks Kyle around his laughter.

"Soft, man. Like Charmin," responds Quentin still laughing. "I forgot you're an old guy," states Quentin before bursting into another fit of laughter.

"Funny yung'un. I bet I can still kick your ass. But enough fun and games, I made sure that word got around the station about our visit your site since Sylvia seems to know every move we make when it comes to Givens. So, hopefully word will get back to Ms Williams and she is ready to make a play on Givens."

"Oh I have no doubt she's ready, but just to make sure I'm going to call my boss and hope that the leak in my team is listening. I'll catch up with you later."

After hanging up with Kyle, Quentin gives Brad a call and lets him know what took place today with Givens and the police. He also lets him know that he won't be in play for the takedown if it happens tonight, just in case something goes wrong.

Less than thirty minutes later, Sylvia gets a call from her contact within the bureau letting her know what has just transpired in Dallas. "I know all about it. My contact on the DPD already called me with the information, and I'm set and ready to go. I just want to know McNair's position in the play."

"As I've already told you, McNair is not a player in this game. In fact, from what I've learned his is the one that actually tipped off the police when his security staff tipped him off about the extra nighttime activities of Charles Givens and his crew. I just hope this is the guy you've been after, I want this whole thing over with. I've never wanted to be a spy, just an efficient administrative assistant."

"You lost someone just like I lost someone, and we both agreed that the person that took them away from us should pay. This was the only way to make it happen," states Sylvia with more than a little tension in her voice.

"I know Sylvia, I know. It's just that sometimes I feel like such a traitor helping you this way since the government cut you lose. I just hope this is the end, and then maybe both of us can get on with our lives."

"I hope so too. I'm actually tired of living like this, but I need closure for Q and the rest of my team. If everything goes as planned, you won't hear from me again after today. So, let me take the time now to say thank you for all you have done for me and my team, and I wish you all the best with the rest of your life. Gotta go." Sylvia disconnects the call before her friend could say another word. She needed to keep her mind clear and focused. She could reminisce about her friend after she completed this one last mission on behalf a country she would soon have to leave behind.

Shut the Game Down

Kyle and his crew are suited and booted, and ready for action. Thanks to Quentin's secret room and passage ways, they are able to position themselves at the site without being seen. They also know that they are not to interfere with Sylvia Williams should she appear on the playing field. The feds have given them clearance to let her handle this situation as she sees fit just so that they can put an end to her clandestine activities.

Charles Givens and his crew have put their plans in motion as well since they don't know what was caught on the site's surveillance cameras. Charles' private jet is fueled and ready for take-off, and his operating room is set-up on the plane so when he lands he will no longer have the face of Charles Givens.

Quentin is at his real estate office ready to watch the play take place on closed circuit monitors connected to every camera on the site, some none of the other players know about.

Sylvia has her game plan down, and her crew at the ready. She can't wait to look into the eyes of the man who killed her team, and most importantly her family and turned her world upside down. The only part of her plan that is not finalized is whether or not she will kill him, or let him take his chances with the court system. "I guess I'll have to play it by ear," she says out loud to herself.

Food From The Heart

*****

As soon as nightfall arrives, everybody goes into motion. Charles and his crew begin loading their merchandise into one of the construction trucks even though they would have preferred to use their own trucks, but they don't want anyone to be able to trace their actual mode of transportation. Once they are away from the site, they will transfer their product into one of their own trucks for delivery to their buyer.

Just as soon as the last crate is loaded on the trucks, Kyle puts his team on first alert on the off chance that Sylvia doesn't show up, or isn't able to handle the situation. Little does he know that Sylvia and her team have been on first alert as soon as the first truck was completely loaded, just on the off chance they were going to move the trucks out one at a time.

"Alright," begins Charles, "everybody knows what they have to do, right?"

"Yes, Boss," is the chorus from his crew. However, the next words out of their mouths are "What the fuck," as Sylvia and her crew surround each and every vehicle with guns at the ready.

"I would advise everyone to take shallow breaths and make no sudden movements," instructs Sylvia as her crew makes their move. "This is not a drill, and each and everyone one of my men are trained snipers and will not hesitate to shoot anyone of you if so much as take a deep breath."

Kyle and his crew whisper a collective "Damn", as Sylvia makes her move. They quickly realize that she doesn't need their help, but they still remain at the ready just in case she's willing to let the law in on a piece of the action.

"Bitch, you . . .," is all Charles is able to get out of his mouth before Sylvia has her Desert Eagle imbedded in his cheek.

"You might want to choose your words carefully, Mr. Givens," begins Sylvia, "as I have an itchy trigger finger and a hair trigger on this weapon." She takes a second to remove her cap and glasses so that she can look directly into his eyes. "I've been waiting three long years for this moment," she states. "This is your last move as a free man, and if you don't cooperate it could be your last move as breathing man. So, if I were you I would carefully plan my next move and my next words." Still looking in his eyes, Sylvia gives her crew their instructions, "Alpha Team disarm and subdue the men you have surrounded." Once they have completed their objective, she gives Teams Bravo, Delta, and Omega the same instructions. Once every member of Charles' crew has been disarmed and detained, she states out loud, "Lieutenant Wright, your men may now retrieve your prisoners since I know you are on the scene."

"How the hell did she know we were here," Kyle asks out loud. However, before anyone can say a word, he gives the order for his crew to move out. "What do you plan to do with him," Kyle asks Sylvia once he has all the prisoners loaded into the transport vehicle.

"He and I are going to go to his office, and have a chat. If I like what he has to say, then we will meet you at the station," she states while never taking her eyes off Charles. "However, if he feeds me some bullshit, you'll never see him or me again. No matter what, it's been a pleasure working with you Kyle, and I wish you the best." She then pulls a second Desert Eagle from her back as she tells Charles to turn around. As he does as asked, she points one at Charles' head while placing the other in his back and they walk towards his office.

Kyle and his crew move out with their prisoners and the cargo. Quentin has been watching the events take place on the security monitors in his office, and is amazed at how efficient Sylvia and her team were when taking down Charles and his crew. Knowing he's going to have to give a full report in the morning to his superiors,

Food From The Heart

Quentin tunes into the events taking place in Charles' office between him and Sylvia.

What Quentin and the others don't know is that Brad, Quentin's superior, is on his way to Dallas as the traitor in the organization has come clean to him. She became overly concerned about what Sylvia would do after their last conversation, and started feeling guilty about the information and supplies that she furnished to Sylvia without anyone's knowledge.

ReGina Crawford

Questions and Answers I

Once inside his office, Sylvia holsters the gun she had placed in Charles' back, and hands him a set of handcuffs telling him to handcuff his hands in front of him. Once the handcuffs are secure she sits him down in one of the guest chairs in front of his desk. She then haves him handcuff each of his legs to the legs of the chair, before she retrieves her second weapon from her back and takes the chair behind his desk.

"Now Mr. Givens, Mr. Red, or whatever your name is, I need you to answer a few questions for me. And let me caution you up front to be honest with me, because I am not in the mood for bullshit after three years of waiting. You've got to know that your career as a gun runner is over, so you might as well tell the truth. Especially since I was telling the truth when I told Lieutenant Wright that if I don't like what I hear no one will see you ever again, and my two friends here Desert and Eagle will make sure of that. And just like you are able to go underground for years and years, I too can go underground. And I will have no problem going underground for the rest of my life after this."

Quentin is watching the exchange when he sees a lone figure approaching his back door. Not expecting anyone, Quentin immediately picks up his Glock 45 off the desk and makes his way to the door while still keeping an eye on the monitor. When the figure is three steps away from the door, he puts his hands in the air and Quentin is able to see what he is holding in his left hand. Immediately relieved, Quentin opens the back door and allows Brad to enter. "What the hell are you doing here," Quentin asks as he grabs his superior in a huge bear hug.

"Long story," begins Brad while returning Quentin's hug, "but the short version is Zakiya told me about what she thought was going to happen tonight and her involvement with Sylvia."

"I'm glad she told you since I was dreading having to drop the dime on her once this was over," states Quentin.

"You knew," shouts Brad.

"I just found out a couple of days ago that she was involved, but we'll have to talk about this later. Sylvia has Charles hostage in his office at the construction site, and we need to watch the events in case she needs our help."

"Why are you watching from here? Don't you think we should be on hand at the site?"

"I don't want her to know who I really am, so I thought that it would be better if I stayed away from the site," answers Quentin.

"You have a mobile monitor right," asks Brad.

"Yes, why?"

"We need to get to the site now. Zakiya thinks that Sylvia is going to kill Charles regardless of what he says to her, and I really don't want that to happen," responds Brad.

"Why," asks Quentin.

"One, I think that Charles could be very useful to us in the future, and two I would hate to put one of our best operatives on the Most Wanted list."

"I don't know if I completely understand, but I'm sure you'll be able to give me the full run down once this over," says Quentin. Not waiting for Brad's response, Quentin activates the mobile monitor and gathers the rest of his gear so that they can leave for the construction site.

*****

Charles remains silent as Sylvia stares at him looking like the devil reincarnate armed and ready for war.

"Silence. Not exactly what I expected from you," comments Sylvia. "If you don't just want to come clean on all your activities, I guess we can play twenty questions," she continues. "Let's start with the most important question first, how did you know about my teams plans to take you down three years ago?"

Charles debates on whether he should tell her anything until she starts attaching a silencer to one of her weapons. "Slow down you crazy bitch," he begins. Sylvia attaches a silencer to her second weapon. "Okay, okay," states a now nervous Charles. "I knew that someone was on to my operation, and was trying to cover my tracks so I had my warehouse rigged to blow to throw whoever it was off track. The death of your squad was simply a bonus, no one knew they would be there. Although, I'm wondering why you weren't there with them as their Capitan."

"That's none of your concern," states Sylvia is a deadly voice. "But how do you know I was their Capitan?"

"When their bodies were found, their fingerprints were taken and your database hacked to find out who they were. I was able to get

Food From The Heart

their names, ranks, and the details of their mission. You were listed as the capitan of the mission they were assigned to, so why weren't you with them?"

"I told you that was none of your business," she states as she leans over the desk with both guns pointed in his direction. "I'm the one asking the questions here," she continues. "Now, I want to know every asshole you've sold guns to. Every one."

"Why is this so important to you? You've been dogging me for six years, and I won't answer another question until I get some answers. You won't kill me until you get everything you're looking for, so I'm not worried about you shooting me," states Charles displaying more bravery than he was actually feeling at the moment.

To answer his question, Sylvia puts a bullet in his right shoulder. Charles screams in pain as the bullet enters his flesh. "Still not worried," she asks.

*****

Quentin and Brad arrive at the site just as Sylvia shoots Charles, "Damn," states Brad out loud. "I was so hoping he wouldn't give her a reason to shoot him. It's going to be difficult to get him to help us if he is filled with holes from those twins she calls friends."

"What do you want to do," asks Quentin. "I still don't want her to know who I am, just in case this isn't the last mission she decides to undertake."

"Don't worry, I'm going to handle this one myself," responds Brad.

"Wait man, you haven't been in the field in over ten years," begins Quentin, "do you think you're ready to take on the likes of Sylvia Williams?"

ReGina Crawford

"What are you trying to say Quentin? You don't think I can handle myself or her?"

"I'm just saying, you've been behind a desk for over ten years and she's been in the field all that time. Hell she's been a rogue agent for three years, and there's no telling what new skills she's picked up in all that time."

"What you don't know is that I take field training every year, so I am up on all the new tactics and am in excellent shape. Don't worry, I've got this."

"If you say so boss," responds Quentin.

Quentin heads to his offices on the site, while Brad makes his way to Charles' office. When he is five feet from the door, Sylvia calls out, "Stop right there Capitan Davidson."

"Shit," whispers Brad angrily as he freezes in his tracks.

"Are you here to apprehend me? Or to help with the interrogation?"

"I'm here to help you Capitan Williams," responds Brad. "I know how important this is to you, and I just want to make sure you don't end up a fugitive after this is over."

Food From The Heart

Unexpected Developments

Not really wanting to go into hiding after this whole ordeal is over with, Sylvia concedes and allows Brad to enter the office. "Come on in Capitan Davidson, but remember this is my interrogation."

Brad enters the office, "Deal", he states. However, he takes a half a second pause as he finally gets an up-close and personal look at the elusive Sylvia Williams. *'Damn, she looks better in person than in any of the photos that I've seen of her,'* he thinks to himself. After making a quick recovery, he takes a stand behind her and allows her to continue her interrogation.

Charles takes advantage of the disruption, and makes a plea to Brad, "Man, this bitch is crazy. Get me out of here."

Sylvia takes another shot at him, but Brad interferes and she misses his other shoulder. Afraid that she might try to shoot him next, Brad places her in a bear hug to keep her from raising either of her friends. What neither one of them is prepared for is the spark of electricity that passes through both of their bodies. Knowing that now is not the right time to investigate that little surprise, Brad looks her in the eyes and says, "We don't need him full of holes when we take him in, so take it easy with your friends there, okay?"

Needing a little more time to recover, it's a minute longer before Sylvia responds. "Fine," she states a little softer than she intended.

ReGina Crawford

"Do you two need a moment alone," Charles asks sarcastically.

They both turn to him with their guns raised, "Don't push your luck," states Brad with deadly intent in his voice. He then turns to Sylvia, "Carry on Capitan," he states as he takes up his previous position behind her chair.

Sylvia returns her attention to her hostage. "Ready to answer my question now," she asks as though there was not a break in the interrogation.

"You're going to let her get away with this," Charles asks Brad. When Brad doesn't respond and Sylvia aims her friends at him again, Charles starts stuttering, "I can't . . . uh . . . just give up . . . the people I've dealt with."

"Yes you can, unless you want another hole in you. I have no problem with it, but you might," comes back Sylvia as she takes aim at his left shoulder again.

"Alright, alright, but what am I going to get for my cooperation?"

"Fewer holes in your body," quips Sylvia.

Charles looks at Brad and seeing that he is not going to get any help from him, he states, "I've sold guns to any and every one who had the money. Iraqis, Saudis, Germans, Asians, Cubans, Columbians, Niggas in the hood. You can't expect me to remember each and every one of them."

"I don't really care about the niggas in the hood, but I am concerned about those who have waged war against American Troops."

Charles runs down every radical military group he's ever sold weapons to, along with the dates and types of weapons sold and any other information he had about their organizations.

Food From The Heart

Once he's dumped his brain, Brad asks Sylvia if he can have a word with her in private. She agrees and they step out into the outer office. "I want to help you as much as I can Sylvia," begins Brad. "We've been wanting to put an end to this guy's gun running as much as you have, and I don't want you to have to go into hiding. So we need to put together a plan of action together to turn him, and make sure you don't end up behind bars yourself."

"What do you have in mind," asks Sylvia a little more breathlessly than she intended.

"Sit down, and let me lay it all out for you."

*****

Once Quentin enters his surveillance room in his offices, he sits back to watch the developments taking place in Charles' office. He's surprised by Brad's reaction to seeing Sylvia for the first time. Never once has he seen his superior affected by the presence of a woman, and especially when on a mission. "Hmm, this could prove to be interesting indeed," states Quentin out loud.

He continues watching the interaction between them, and is surprised to see the sparks fly when Brad places her in a bear hug to keep her from putting another bullet into Charles Givens. "I can't wait to find out what that was all about when this over," comments Quentin to the empty room.

He takes a full report of all of the people that Charles has sold guns to as he rattles them off to Brad and Sylvia. The list is long and varied, however, it will help them with future missions. Not wanting to give up his cover, Quentin takes the cue from Brad to leave the site as he takes Sylvia out to the outer office to finalize their plans for turning Charles in to the authorities.

ReGina Crawford

After outlining the plan to Sylvia, Brad calls in transport for Charles. Once they arrive in Washington with their prisoner, Brad escorts Sylvia to his office while MPs take Charles to the infirmary to have his wound treated.

"Have a seat Capitan," Brad tells Sylvia. "First, I would like to congratulate you on the success of this mission. You have proven to be a first rate soldier. However, there will be some sanctions against you as this mission was not authorized by any government official, and your little help mate will also find herself punished for her part in your activities."

"Wait just one damn minute," yells Sylvia as she jumps to her feet and touches her nose to Brad's. "You said you weren't there to apprehend me. I should have known better than to trust a paper pusher like you to do the right thing," she continues. However, that damn spark flares up between them again, so she pulls back and starts pacing the room as she puts together a plan to get out of his office and out of the country. Everything is already in place for her life in hiding, she just has to get to her boat in the gulf.

"I'm not letting you out of here Sylvia, so stop running options in that head of yours," he states. Undeterred by the angry look she sends his way, he continues, "You will not be doing any jail time for this, but you will have to resume your role as an operative for the government," he stops speaking as she turns to him with fire flashing in her eyes. "It's the only way, I can let you get away with everything you've done for the past three years and for stealing government property and funds."

Sylvia walks around his desk to confront him face-to-face, and when Brad sees her intent, he immediately stands so as not to give her an advantage. "If the government hadn't abandoned me, I wouldn't

Food From The Heart

have had to "steal" anything. Zakiya wouldn't have felt compelled to help me, and she wouldn't be in trouble right now."

Brad is overwhelmed by her presence and fire, and reacts without thinking. He grabs her in a bear hug and takes the kiss he's being dying to take since first laying eyes on her. Sylvia is first stunned by the kiss, then overwhelmed by the electricity passing between them. Before she knows it, she's returning the kiss whole heartedly. Once the need to breathe becomes paramount, Brad breaks the kiss. "I'm sorry," states Brad. After a few more gulps of air, he continues, "No I'm not. I've been wanting to kiss you from the moment I laid eyes on you tonight." He feels her fighting against his hold on her, but refuses to let her go. "I would let you go, but I'm afraid you might shoot me."

"They took my guns when we entered the building, remember," responds Sylvia still trying to regain control of her breathing.

"You got me on that one, but I'm still not letting you go. I know you are deadly even without a weapon in hand, and I really don't want to fight you right now. I'd rather make love to you, but somehow I don't think you'll let me."

"Are you sure about that," asks Sylvia breathing a little more steadily now. But his hold on her, and his words are making her head spin and her heart race. She's not sure what to do since she hasn't been this affected by a man since Qasean.

New Beginnings

Quickly recovering from the shock of her response, Brad kisses her deeply one more time. When he's finally able to break the kiss, he lets her go and quickly moves away from her and braces himself for any assault she may decide to make.

To his surprise, Sylvia simply takes her seat as she tries to recover from his touch and his kisses. "Sit down Brad. You are in no danger from me. At least not at the moment."

Brad eases into his seat still on alert. "Look Sylvia, I know you weren't expecting me to attack you that way and it certainly wasn't planned on my part, but I don't regret one second of it. But that's not why I brought you here. I want to make sure that we have an agreement before I take you to the General for him to give you the details of your new position."
"Brad, you might be surprised to hear this, but I have no more fight left in me. This mission has been my life for the last three years, and I was prepared to go into hiding after it was over and live a life of leisure. I don't want to be a field agent anymore."

"And you won't be."

"What? Wait a minute. I know you don't think I'd be happy as a paper pusher do you?"

Food From The Heart

"No Sylvia, I know you won't be happy behind a desk, but I think you will be happy as a trainer and consultant."

"What?"

"Your new position involves you training recruits that have been assigned to clandestine missions so that they will know how to survive in the wild, and especially if they get disconnected from their team. Plus, you will serve as a consultant when those missions are being planned, helping with the strategy and attack methods. I think you'll be very happy in that position. You'll even get to travel."

"I don't know Brad."

"You don't have a choice Sylvia. It's the only way to save your hide and Zakiya's."

"Shit," curses Sylvia. She leans her head back and closes her eyes to digest what Brad has just told her.

Brad, in the meantime, is studying the length of her neck and fantasying about placing kisses down that neck as well as other places on her body. As his arousal becomes uncomfortable, he shifts in his chair which makes Sylvia look in his direction. He is unable to mask the desire in his eyes, and he notes the surprise in hers. He cocks his eyebrow at her, before shyly smiling. He knows that his reaction is a surprise to her, and frankly it's a surprise to him as well.

"How closely will we be working together," she asks.

"If I have my way, we'll be working very closely together."

"I mean in my new position," clarifies Sylvia.

"I am talking about your new position," he responds with more than a little subjectiveness in his voice.

"I'm serious here Brad."

"I am too," he responds.

Sylvia rolls her eyes before closing them again, and is saved from having to respond as Brad's phone rings. "Yeah," he barks into the phone.

"Interrupting, am I," quips Quentin on the other end of the phone.

"As a matter of fact you are," Brad barks.

"Take it easy," quips Quentin. "I was just checking in."

"Check in tomorrow," states Brad, and then he promptly hangs up the phone.

Quentin bursts into a fit of laughter as he hangs up. He then calls Quintana to give her the update. "Hey Sweetheart," he says when she picks up the phone. "It's over, and Sylvia is safe and sound."

"Are you serious? What happened?"

"How about I tell you over a bottle of champagne while relaxing in the hot tub?"

"Sounds good. I'll be there in thirty minutes."

"I'll be waiting."

*****

"It's been a long day. Let's get you checked into your temporary quarters," states Brad.

Food From The Heart

Sylvia doesn't say a word. She simply gets up from the chair, and lets Brad lead her out of his office and out of the building. She does, however, retrieve her friends on the way out.

Once they arrive at the safe house that Brad has arranged for, he tells her to go get a bath while he sees what there is to eat. Still pondering the events that took place in Brad's office, Sylvia makes her way to the bathroom and takes the suggested bath. Twenty minutes later, Brad enters the bathroom with a nightgown and robe, as well as, a glass of white wine. Sylvia doesn't acknowledge his presence, hoping he'll turn around and leave.

"I know you know I'm here, and I'm not leaving so you might as well open your eyes."

"Why can't you just be a gentleman and leave?"

"Because I don't want to be a gentleman. I want to make love to you." Sylvia's eyes pop open at his comment, but before she can say a word he hands her the glass of wine. "This should help you relax, as well as, the fact that I'm not going to make love to you tonight since I don't think you're up to it. There'll be plenty of time for that." After she takes the glass from his hand, he makes his way to the door throwing over his shoulder, "Your nightgown and robe are draped across the commode."

"What the hell is wrong with me," Sylvia asks out loud once Brad has left. "I've never been this affected by the presence of a man, not even my beloved Qasean. She takes a deep drink from the glass before sitting it on the floor, and leaning back against the back of the tub.

ReGina Crawford

Compliments To The Chef

Another thirty minutes have gone by, and Sylvia hasn't emerged from the bathroom. Brad wonders if she escaped out the window, or drowned herself in the tub. "Only one way to find out," he states out loud as he makes his way to the bathroom. He pauses just inside the door, Sylvia looks like a complete angel sleeping in the tub, a very desirable angel since all of her bubbles have dissipated and he has a clear view of every inch of her voluptuous frame. After looking his fill, he scoops her up in his arms and carriers her to her room. He can't resist taking one last look at her before covering her with the sheet. "She's probably going to be mad as hell that I put her to bed wet, but if I dried her off I'd be in that bed with her and we wouldn't be sleeping," he states as he pours himself a drink in the sitting area.

Sylvia wakes up ten minutes later as she notices she is no longer floating in water. It takes her a minute to remember where she is, but once she does she takes note of the fact that she is in bed completely nude and there is only one way she got there. Letting her anger get the best of her, she quickly gets out of the bed and marches into the sitting area to give Brad a piece of her mind. "You had no right to remove me from the tub. I have no intentions on drowning myself," she rants as she enters the sitting area. "I will not be treated like a child," she continues.

Displaying an outward calm he is far from feeling, Brad takes a sip of his drink to keep from tasting her skin, "Believe me Sylvia, I have

Food From The Heart

no intentions of treating you like a child. As a matter of fact, if you continue to stand there as bare as the day you were born, I may show you exactly how I plan to treat you. Right here. Right now."

"You cannot intimidate me with your sexual innuendos. As a matter of fact, if you lay one finger on me you'll . . .," her voice falters as Brad leaves the chair and is a hair's breath away from her.

"I'll what Sylvia," asks Brad standing nose-to-nose with her. The manly scent of him, the heat of his body temporarily disorients her, and she is unable to finish what she was about to say. Brad takes her silence as acquiescence, and takes control of her mouth with his. She returns his kiss without hesitation, and Brad takes that as her consent to let him love her.

He carries her to his bed, and tastes every inch of her bare skin. Her moans of pleasure only add fuel to his fire, and the scream of her climax nearly does him in. He quickly removes his clothes as she rides out the climax, and then rejoins her on the bed. If his suspicions are right, she hasn't made love since the death of her fiancé, and he knows he's going to have to take it easy with her this first time. He slowly kisses her breasts before making his way slowly down the rest of her body. He knows he has to get control of himself, so he makes love to her with his mouth again to calm himself down. While she is riding out the waves of her second climax, he makes his first tentative entrance into her depths. Even as wet as she is from his mouth and her first two orgasms, he is not able to penetrate her fully. He pulls back and makes another attempt, but he is still unable to achieve full penetration. On his third attempt, he is finally able to bury himself to the hilt inside of her. He becomes so overwhelmed by the sensation of being inside her he freezes as he tries to adjust himself to what he's feeling.

"Don't stop now," whispers Sylvia. "Please," she pleads a few seconds later.

"I have no intentions on stopping Sylvia. I just want to savor being inside you," he replies. "You have no idea what being inside you is doing to me right now," he adds.

"If you being inside me is affecting you the same way it's affecting me, then I think I have a pretty good idea how you feel," is her response.

Her response breaks his control, and he begins moving in and out of her at a frantic pace. The moans and sighs that escape each of their lips sends them both into overdrive, and the pace of their love making gets faster and faster. Her scream of ecstasy mingles with his roar of completion as a powerful orgasm slams into both of them at the same time. Neither of them are able to move or speak for quite some time as they try to calm their racing hearts and labored breathing.

Brad is the first one to regain his voice, "I didn't want our first time to be like that," he begins. "It was supposed to be slow and easy not hard and frantic."

"I didn't want slow and easy," states Sylvia. "I needed hard and frantic," she adds before taking a deep breath. "This is the first time I've felt alive in three years," she states before breaking down in tears. Brad cradles her in his arms and rocks her as she cries. Once the tears are almost over, she asks, "What am I going to do now?"

"What do mean," asks Brad.

"Qasean and my team and our missions were my life. When I lost them, finding their killer became my life," she begins. "That's over now, and I have nothing to drive me. Nothing to live for," she states as she lays her head on his shoulder and starts crying again.

Not wanting her know how much her words angered him, he pulls her closer and rocks her in his arms. After giving her a few

Food From The Heart

moments to let her tears free fall, he lifts her head and looks her straight in the eyes, "You do have something to live for," he states in a voice that sounded a lot angrier than he intended. He takes a deep breath, and begins again, "I know this might sound crazy, but I love you and I'm not letting you go." She starts to shake her head, and he grabs her chin. "I do love you. I don't know why or how, but I do. Please, just don't walk away from me. Give us a chance."

"I'm scared, Brad."

"I know sweetheart, I'm scared too. I've never been in love in my life," he states. At her surprised look he adds, "No woman has ever moved me the way that you do, and no woman has ever moved me the first time I laid eyes on her."

Not knowing what to say, Sylvia simply kisses him senseless and they make love into the wee hours of the morning.

*****

Quintana arrives at Quentin's exactly thirty minutes later. Quentin greets her at the door completely nude with two glasses of champagne in his hands. "Right on time, sweetheart," he states as she closes the door. "Now get undressed, the hot tub is waiting."

Quintana strips right in front of the door, takes her glass of champagne and follows Quentin to the hot tub. He relates the evening's events to her with her cradled between his legs as the water swirls and bubbles around them.

"You think that Brad is making a move on Sylvia," asks Quintana as Quentin ends his story with the phone call he made to Brad once he arrived home.

"I know Brad is making a move on Sylvia. The question is, how is she going to respond?"

"Very true. Very true indeed since I don't think she's been with anyone since Qasean died. This could prove to be a very interesting development," ponders Quintana out loud.

"Well enough about them. How about I make a move on you," quips Quentin.

"Why don't you give it a try, and see what happens?"

"In a playful mood are we," asks Quentin before scooping her up in his arms. He ignores her yelp of surprise, and carries her to the blanket he has spread before the fireplace. "Let's see how you like this," he states as he buries his face between her legs.

After her third climax, she grabs his head and pulls him up. "Why . . . do I . . . always . . . have to . . . drag . . . your mouth . . . from my . . . body," ask Quintana as she struggles to catch her breath.

Laughing, Quentin responds, "You shouldn't serve such a first class meal." He then kisses her navel before saying, "My compliments to the chef."

Quintana laughs before flipping him over on his back, "My turn," she states before taking him inside her hot wet mouth.

"Oh shit," is all Quentin can say as she makes love to him with her mouth. Next word he screams is her name as a powerful orgasm hits him some time later. Once he's able to speak again, he says, "That was not the way I wanted to cum."

"But you enjoyed it."

"Without a doubt."

"Then what are you whining about?"

Food From The Heart

Quentin doesn't say a word, he just pulls her up his body and kisses her senseless before flipping her on her back. He then proceeds to treat her to two more orgasms with his mouth before loving her completely with his body.

ReGina Crawford

Making Amends

Brad wakes up several hours later after making love to Sylvia all night, and makes a few phone calls. Once she wakes up he lets her know that everything is in place for her professionally, and that he plans to take of her personally. He is surprised at how quickly she accepts, but doesn't question her decision.

At noon he receives a call from Quentin, "What's up," he answers the phone.

"You tell me man. You sounded quite busy last night, but you seem to have survived the night. Guess the lady didn't do you in," states Quentin trying to keep the laughter out of his voice.

"No, the lady didn't do me in the way you think," states Brad not trying to hide the laughter in his voice while winking at the smile that Sylvia has on her face.

"Sounds like an interesting story. One you'll have to tell me about when you don't have an audience. I just wanted to make sure everything ended as planned last night."

"Everything is as it should be. No worries."

"Glad to hear it. We'll talk tomorrow."

Food From The Heart

"Yes we will," responds Brad before hanging up the phone.

After talking with Brad, Quentin and Quintana head over to Indigo's to check in with Kyle. "What's up Bro," states Quentin as Kyle opens the door.

"Not much man," he states as he grabs Quentin in a brotherly hug. "Glad everything went off without a hitch last night. Our special guests from last night were whisked off to Washington as soon as they were finished being processed."

Just as he finished talking, in walks Indigo with her *your-lucky-you-weren't-involved* look on her face. Quentin puts his hands in the air in surrender before stating, "I wasn't even close to the action."

"I know," responds Indigo, "Just make sure you keep it that way. Now give me my hug." Quentin hugs her, and then Indigo moves on to hug Quintana. "I know you're glad it's over too. How did your friend Sylvia fare in all the action?"

"From what I hear, everything turned out even better than she expected," answers Quintana while cutting a look at Quentin.

"What was that," asks Kyle and Indigo at the same time.

"It seems my superior had some life altering plans for Sylvia last night after all the action was over," responds Quentin.

"Oh really," quips Kyle, "And what was the lady's take on those plans?"

"From the brief report I got this afternoon, she wasn't opposed to them."

"I'll be damned," states Indigo, "I thought the lady would be on the first thing smoking that would get her as far away from everyone as possible."

"I think those were her plans, however, I think Brad convinced her to stay around," responds Quentin.

The next thing they know there is a knock on the door. Kyle answers the door to find Keith, Jade, Kendrick, and Ebony on his door step. "Looks like the gangs all here," he says over his shoulder as the entourage enters the house.

Once Keith spies Quintana, he asks, "Did these two thugs eat all the grub before we got here?"

"There was no grub," retorts Quentin.

"How is the number one chef in Dallas in the house, and there's no grub," asks Keith.

"Because we just got here. Because we don't live here. Because she's not your personal chef. Need any more reasons," asks Quentin trying not to smile.

"What's the puppy yipping about," Keith asks Kyle.

"You know puppy's, always trying to prove to the Big Dogs they're ready to run," quips Kyle.

Seeing the way Quentin was glaring at the both of them, Quintana decides to intervene, "Why don't we go to the restaurant for a late brunch?"

"A woman with a good head on her shoulders, and cooks like a dream," quips Kendrick. "Who's driving," he then asks.

The group loads up into Keith and Kendrick's SUVs, and head to the restaurant. Just as they are about to walk in the door, who is walking in their direction? None other than Brad and Sylvia, both smiling

Food From The Heart

ear-to-ear. Quentin is praying that Brad doesn't acknowledge him since that would give him away. He has nothing to worry about as Brad notices the large group standing in front of the restaurant. Sylvia greets them all, and introduces Brad.

Kyle then invites them to have brunch with their group. "We would love to," replies Brad. "Sylvia tells me that you helped with the sting last night."

"Yes sir, we did."

"Did a good job too from what I hear."

"We'd like to think so," states Keith. "But I don't want to talk shop, I want to eat the incredible meal that is waiting on me in side."

"Then follow me," states Quintana.

"Ana," begins Sylvia, "can I talk to you for a minute?"

"Sure." Quintana then turns to her hostess and lets her know to add two more settings to her table, and that she would be right there. "I'm glad this is over for you, and that you're okay," states Quintana as she turns back to Sylvia.

"Are you really?"

"Of course. Why wouldn't I be?"

"You don't think I'm betraying Q by being with Brad?"

"Honey, we lost Qasean three years ago. You have mourned his loss long enough. I've always wanted nothing but the best for you, and you know it. Be happy."

"I am," responds Sylvia.

"You sound surprised by that."

"I am. I've been so driven by finding his killer that I never took a close look at my personal life. That's not true. I actually felt like I had no life after I lost him, but Brad has convinced me that I do have a personal life and a new professional life thanks to his connections with the government."

"That's great Sylvia," states Quintana as she gives her friend a big hug. "Will you be moving to Washington?"

"Yes, I will. I'll make the announcement at brunch. Now let's go join the others." The ladies walk to the table hand-in-hand.

"Where's Quentin," asks Quintana when they reach the table.

"He's in your kitchen," replies Indigo. "Said he had some special instructions for the cook." Just as Quintana heads toward the kitchen, Indigo grabs her hand, "And he said you were not allowed to interfere." Quintana raises an eyebrow at Indigo, and Indigo raises one in return.

Quintana takes the cue and takes her seat that the table, "I'm sure he can do no harm in there. My cooks know how to take care of themselves."

Food From The Heart

Next Life Time

When Quentin returns to the table, he has a mischievous grin on his face as he takes his seat and places a kiss on Quintana's cheek. "What have you been up to in my kitchen," Quintana asks Quentin.

"I had a special request for the chef."

"Does your request involve fresh oysters?"

"You really know how to ruin a surprise," pouts Quentin.

"Aww Honey, I'm sorry," quips Quintana around a smile.

"You're not sorry," Quentin continues to pout.

Quintana leans over and whispers in his ear, "I'll show you just how sorry I am when I get you home later." Then she sucks on his earlobe to give him a slight preview of what he was in for.

The sensation of her mouth on his ear sends chills down his spine, and he closes his eyes and bites his lip to keep from embarrassing himself at the table. A few seconds later, he whispers in her ear, "You'll pay for that later, as well as, show me how sorry you are for ruining my surprise."

Kyle and Keith clear their throats at the same time to remind Q squared, as they call them, that they are not alone.

"Why is everything always in stereo when you two are together," Quentin asks the duo.

"Great minds think alike," they both speak at the same time.

"See there it goes again," states Quentin. The whole table bursts out laughing.

Just as the laughter dies down, the server brings out the appetizers for the group. Quentin picks up one of the oysters, and asks Quintana to feed it to him. She takes the oyster from his hand, and catches her breath at the large diamond ring nestled inside. Taking advantage of her speechless state, Quentin asks, "Will you marry me, and be my partner in life and love?"

Tears immediately stream down Quintana's face as she whispers yes, before shouting it loud enough for the whole restaurant to hear. The restaurant is suddenly completely quiet. The staff on duty immediately figures out what's going on, and all start cheering. Then the restaurants patrons start cheering as well. Quentin places the ring on Quintana's finger, and they give each other a promise sealing kiss.

Once all the excitement dies down and everyone goes back to their lunch, Sylvia leans over to Quentin and asks him if she can talk to him privately.

Quentin nods his head in agreement as his curiosity gets the best of him. They get up from the table and head towards the lobby of the restaurant followed by the curious stares of the rest of the table.

"What can I do for you Ms Williams," asks Quentin in a not so friendly voice as they reach the lobby.

Food From The Heart

Undeterred by the slight hostility that she hears in his voice, Sylvia replies, "I would like to call a truce between us." Still undeterred by the skeptical cocking of his eyebrow, she continues, "I'm sorry that I suspected you as a possible adversary to my mission. Now that it is over, I realize that you are who you say you are and I would like for us to at least be civil with each other. Especially since you are about to marry my best friend."

"I'm glad to hear that you have changed your mind about me, and I guess we can put the past behind us," responds Quentin. He then adds, "I hope that you will be happy with your new life, and try to stay out of trouble." The smile on his face takes the sting out of his last words, and Sylvia smiles back as she extends her hand to seal their truce. Quentin shakes her hand then leads her back to the table to join the others.

Once they take their seats, Quintana leans over and asks Quentin what happened between him and Sylvia. "We called a truce," he whispers in her ear. Quintana smiles and leans over to kiss him on the cheek, but he turns his face to her and takes the kiss full on the lips. The kiss heats up quickly, and goes on so long that the table at large clears their throats to remind the two that they are not alone. Sheepishly Quentin mutters, "Sorry bout that. I kinda got carried away."

"We could tell," states Kyle and Keith at the same time.

"There goes that stereo thing again," quips Quentin, and the table at large bursts out laughing.

Once the laughter dies down, Kyle asks Brad what brings him and Sylvia back to Dallas. "Sylvia had some unfinished business to conclude," responds Brad while looking pointedly at Sylvia.

"I just wanted to tell you and your men thank you for allowing me to take down Charles, and to apologize for being such a pain in the ass while I was here in the city," states Sylvia as the whole table looks her way.

"You're welcome," states Kyle. "No apology needed though," he adds. "We knew what this case meant to you, and you provided us with information that probably would have taken us a lot longer to get if we had to deal with department red tape."

"I know you're right about the red tape, but I still feel like I could have been a little less hostile to you and your men," responds Sylvia.

"She was a real pain in the ass sometimes," comments Keith. The table looks at him with censure, and he responds, "What? She said the same thing, and no one looked at her sideways."

"That was different," states Jade. "She can say it. You can't," adds Jade looking more than a little pissed with him.

"I don't see what the difference is," begins Keith, but at the look Jade sends his way he changes his tune. "I'm sorry Ms Williams. I didn't mean to sound ungrateful."

Sylvia smiles in his direction, "No harm done since I know you were just stating the truth." She then turns to Quintana, "Ana, I want to thank you for staying my friend throughout all this. I know it was hard for you, and hope I didn't cause you too much heartache while I pursued what had become my life's mission."

"Sylvia, I love you and will always love you. I know how what happened all those years ago destroyed your life as you knew it, and I knew you needed closure. I'm glad you have it, and I wish you all the best as you start your next life."

The ladies have tears in their eyes, and the men interfere as they don't relish the thought of having to deal with a table full of crying women. "What's with the service in this place today," asks Keith.

Food From The Heart

"Yeah, where's my food, I'm hungry," chimes in Kyle.

Before Quintana can say a word, their waitress arrives with their meals. Quentin takes the moment to place a shrimp in her mouth to keep her from lashing out Kyle and Keith. Kyle and Keith follow his lead, and do the same thing to Indigo and Jade.

"That's what I'm talkin bout," states Keith and Kyle at the same time as they take a bite of their food.

"Can someone please turn off the surround sound," quips Quentin, and the whole table bursts out laughing again.

Once the laughter dies down, they finish their lunch, and then each of the couples head their separate ways to enjoy the rest of their day.

Epilogue

When Quentin and Quintana get back to his place, he grabs her around the waist just as he closes the door behind her. "Now, about that hot sexy mouth of yours," he whispers in her ear before taking it into his mouth and suckling. He feels the shiver that runs through her body at the feel of his mouth on her ear, and moves his mouth from her ear to her neck. She grips him tighter as a heated sigh leaves her lips. Quentin carries her over to the couch, and sits down with her on his lap.

After a few more minutes of driving her crazy with his lips and tongue, he looks her in the face until she is able to open her eyes. When she sees the love he has for her shining in his eyes, tears fall from her eyes as she states, "I love you Quentin McNair, and I can't wait to begin my next life time with you."

Quentin pulls her closer to his heart as he kisses the tears from her face. "You have no idea what that means me to me," he states as he kisses the last tear from her cheek.

"You have no idea what you mean to me," she states as she stands as proceeds to do a strip tease.

"What are you doing," asks Quentin already aroused and all she has taken off is her jacket.

Food From The Heart

"Showing you how sorry I am for ruining your surprise," she states as she removes her blouse to reveal a see-through green lace bra. As Quentin makes a move to get up, Quintana puts her foot to his chest and states, "Keep your seat sailor, I'm not finished with my apology yet."

Stunned by this, Quentin keeps his seat and finishes watching the rest of the show. Next comes off Quintana's skirt to reveal a matching see-through lace thong topped off by a black lace garter belt attached to her black sheer thigh high stockings. The picture is completed by her four inch mid-calf strappy black sandals. Quentin is squirming is his seat, as well as, clenching his hands into fist to keep from reaching out and grabbing her. Quintana then proceeds to perform a little belly dance routine for him that has his pants becoming extremely tight in the crotch area as his erection continues to grow.

After a few more minutes of watching her dance, Quentin can't take it anymore and reaches out and grasps her hips as she moves closer to him. "Apology accepted," he practically groans in her ear as he pulls her down on his lap. The contact is too much for him, and he lets out what sounds like a pain-filled groan. However, before Quintana could say a word, Quentin jumps up from the couch still holding her in his arms, and heads to his bedroom. Once he lays her on the bed, she is able to see what the groan was all about. As Quentin removes his jacket, Quintana gets on her knees on the bed, and proceeds to unbuckle his belt. "What are you doing," asks Quentin as he unbuttons his shirt.

"It seems to me that you're in need of my special brand of first-aid," she quips around a smile as she continues to remove his pants.

"Quintana," begins Quentin. "Oh shit," are the next words to come out of his mouth as Quintana begins to administer her own brand of first-aid.

Several hours later, they are both trying to regain control of their breathing and their heart rates when Quintana says, "Thanks for not being hostile to Sylvia today."

"Where did that come from? I know you are not lying here in my arms thinking about a woman," asks Quentin trying not to crack a smile.

Quintana is a little confused at first, then she remembers a prior conversation that they had about Sylvia. She bursts out laughing before saying, "Very funny Quentin. I was just laying here thinking how happy am to have you, and wishing the same thing for her," she begins. "Then it occurred to me that you were actually pretty cordial to her this afternoon at the restaurant."
"I harbor no ill feelings towards Sylvia. I know what she was trying to do, I just felt that there was a better way to handle it than the route she was taking."

"I'm still proud of you," states Quintana before placing a kiss on his lips.

"I'm proud of you too," he states when the kiss ends. She arches an eyebrow in his direction at his words, and he continues, "You didn't abandon her even though you didn't agree with what she was doing, and I think that meant a lot to her. You were her only link to sanity that she had left."

"You are such a special man."

"And you are a special lady, now get some rest while you can," he states as he wraps her in his arms to take a short nap before the loving begins again.

Heart Body and Soul

Turn the page for a sneak peak at the next novel from Ms. Crawford. Expected release date late summer to early fall 2009.

ReGina Crawford

Instant Passion

Having never thrown caution to the wind before, Zamora decides to give in. Maybe this is just what I need to feel alive again. I won't have to worry about looking Nana in the face knowing that I am no longer a virgin without the benefit of marriage. "Okay, as long as we both agree that we will never seek each other out again after this."

He walks over to her and pulls her into his arms, "You have a deal," he states before lowering his mouth to hers. The sensations overwhelm the both of them, and he picks her up and carries her to his bedroom. True to his word, he begins stripping her out of her clothes. First her suit jacket is removed and laid over the back of a chair, then he slowly unbuttons her blouse placing hot little kisses on her neck, chest and stomach. Once he pushes the blouse off her shoulders, he kisses her collar bone, shoulders, and the swells of her breasts above her lavender colored ultra sheer bra. He then flicks his tongue over the turgid points of her nipples before removing her bra, at which point he tests their weight in his hands. He has large hands and her breasts completely fill them, and he is in heaven. He dips his head and takes one peak in his mouth to suckle. Her head falls back and a ragged moan slips through her lips. The sound encourages him to take the other peak into his mouth, and her continued moans are almost his undoing.

Heart Body and Soul

Not wanting to spill his seed inside his pants, he releases her breasts much to her objection and gets down on his knees as he unzips her skirt. Once the skirt pools at her feet, he helps her to step out of it and places it across the chair with her other clothing. He follows the line of her long legs up to the center of her which is barely covered by the lavender thong she is wearing, and has to close his eyes to regain control of the situation. Unfortunately, he takes a deep breath to steady his breathing and inhales the aroused scent of her which is causing his already straining member to press even harder against the front of his pants. Unable to hold back any longer, he reaches out and touches her between her legs. "You're wet," he says in a desire laden voice.

"More like drenched," she responds breathlessly as he continues to caress her through her thong. Unable to resist his touch, she spreads her legs wider to give him better access to her. At which point he slides a finger under the edge of her thong to caress her wet flesh, and an "Oh God," hisses from between her lips at his initial touch. She begins to tremble as her orgasm is fast approaching, "Marquise . . ."

"Yes baby, that's my name. Say it again."

"I'm about to cum," are the next words out of her mouth.

"Then let's get this first one out of the way," he responds while thinking it must have been sometime since she's been with a man since she's climaxing so quickly. Then all thought is gone as she yells out his name as her orgasm crashes down on her. "That's it baby. Just let it go. I promise you there will be more." As she rides out the final notes of her orgasm, he removes the thong, shoes and thigh high stockings. He lays her across the bed, and then begins removing his clothing. Once he is undressed, he climbs onto the foot of the bed and begins kissing his way up her legs from her ankles steadily spreading her thighs wider and wider to accommodate the width of his body. Once he is settled between her thighs, he slowly runs his tongue across the center of her. She

3

arches her hips up off the bed and closer to his mouth, and he takes full advantage of her position by taking her fully into his mouth.

"Marquise," she screams while clutching the sheets on the bed as her hips arch higher.

"Easy," he whispers while placing a hand on her stomach to keep her from going anywhere. "Easy," he whispers again letting his warm breath caress her. He then goes back to enjoying the taste of her. When he feels her ready to climax again, he whispers, "Let go baby. Feed me your love." Once his mouth touches her again, the orgasm crashes over her like tidal waves and she's screaming his name once again.

As she rides out this second orgasm, he covers himself with a condom from the nightstand drawer before rejoining her on the bed. Once she's breathing regularly again, he eases between her thighs and guides himself into her hot silky sheath. He meets resistance, so he withdraws and makes another attempt. Still more resistance, and this time he's sure it's not because it's been a while since she's made love. It hits him like a ton of bricks, she's a virgin. Damn! "Why didn't you tell me," he asks.

"Would it have made a difference," she asks in return.

"Hell yes it would have made a difference," he responds.

"Why? It's no big deal."

"Why? How can you ask why? Sweetheart, you waited this long to be intimate with a man, so I would say that it is a very big deal. Now, why didn't you tell me?"

"I need to have a connection to someone who is alive, and you are the person I've chosen. Plain and simple."

Heart Body and Soul

"There is nothing plain and simple about what we are about to do, believe that. And I believe that there is still something that you're not telling me." Tired of talking, Zamora arches her hips closer to him. The feel of her moving beneath him drains all thoughts from his mind, and his body takes over as he surges forward through the barrier separating him from her womb. He growls "Yes", as she releases a quick scream of pain as he buries himself to the hilt inside of her. Knowing this is her first time, he holds himself still giving her time to get past the pain of losing her virginity. "You okay," he asks after a few moments.

"I'm wonderful, but what are you waiting for," she asks as she flexes her inner walls around him.

The caress sends him over the edge, and he withdraws before surging forward once again. She quickly picks up on his rhythm and moves with him in the age old dance of man and woman. Their moans and sighs of pleasure fill the room as they frantically move to their destination of total fulfillment. The clutching of his manhood by her satin walls lets him know that she is ready to climax, and that knowledge brings him closer to his release. He grips her hips in a tight embrace and strokes her for all she's worth. He can tell that this orgasm is more powerful than the first two, and that she is trying to run from it. "Don't fight it," is his hoarsely stated plea, "Come with me."

She follows his lead, and her climax has her screaming long and loud. His growl of pleasure as he finds his release mingles with her screams. Spent, he collapses on top of her, unable to move. Knowing that he must be crushing her, he rolls onto his side pulling her with him since he wants to stay connected to her.

Once his breathing returns to normal, he opens his eyes and finds that her eyes are still closed but she is wearing the most beautiful smile he has ever seen. "How are you," he whispers not wanting to startle her.

"There are no words to describe how I feel," she whispers her answer as she opens her eyes.

"I feel the same way. I have never felt anything that powerful before," he responds.

She closes her eyes and moans as an aftershock hits her, and she grips him as he is still inside her body. "Hmm," she moans at the feel of him.

"Be careful," he states. She intentionally squeezes him once again. "I don't think you know what you're asking for," he states. She squeezes him once again. "Remember you asked for it," he states as he feels himself lengthening inside her once again. He covers himself with a new condom before pulling her on top of him. At the question in her eyes, he guides her down on his throbbing manhood then grips her hips to show her how to move. She picks up quickly and begins moving on her own, sending his senses spiraling out of control. As she rotates her hips around him, he can take no more and quickly flips her onto her back never breaking the contact of their bodies. He then places her legs over his shoulders to give him greater access, and takes her on the ride of her life. Their labored breathing and skin making contact with skin are the only sounds to be heard throughout the room.

"Oh God," moans Zamora as her climax quickly approaches.

"Almost there," he growls in her ear.

"Yesssss," she screams as her orgasm hits her.

"Zamoraaaaa," he yells as he finds release once again. His body feels like rubber after both of his powerful releases, and once again he collapses on top of her. "Just let me catch my breath, and then I'll move," he whispers.

Heart Body and Soul

"You're just fine where you are," she responds while gasping for air.

Moments later, he rolls onto his side disconnecting his body from hers. She moans a protest at the loss of his body. He chuckles while still trying to regain control of he rapid beating of his heart and his breathing. "Lady, you are going to be the death of me," Marquise states some time later.

"What did I do," she asks.

"You know what you did."

"I have no idea what you're talking about. I'm a novice at this remember."

"That's right," he responds as he opens his eyes to look at her beautiful face. "But you're a fast learner, and I know you know that you have stolen every ounce of my energy."

"I know no such thing," she replies around her smile.

They lay there basking in the aftermath of their love making for another ten minutes before Marquise suggest that they get a shower. After finishing in the shower, they both dress silently knowing that their time together is about to come to an end.

As they reach her car, he reaches into his shirt pocket, and extracts a business card to hand to her. At her questioning look, "I know we said we would probably never see each other again, but just in case you want to get in touch with me take my card. My cell number is written on the back of the card." She starts to shake her head no, but he thrusts the card at her anyway. "Please, just take it. Even if you throw it away later, take it now."

She takes the card and places it inside her purse before turning back to him to give him one last kiss before she walks away from him forever. He doesn't try to detain her, he merely watches as she gets in her car and drives away out of his life. He's still standing there ten minutes after her tails lights have faded from sight. What is he supposed to do now? He has no idea, so he heads back inside the house since he wasn't officially on duty anyway today. He was just simply monitoring that stretch of highway in hopes that he would see the one that got away, and even though he captured her for a couple of hours she got away again this time taking more than just his pride. She took his soul.

Once she has put some distance between herself and Marquise, Zamora pulls off the highway into a rest area. She pulls his card out of her purse with every intention of throwing it in the trash, but she is unable to let the card go so she simply throws it into her glove box. With that done, she lays her head against the headrest and closes her eyes trying to regain some semblance of composure before she gets back on the highway. She wonders how long it will take the feel of him, the smell of him, the sound of him, the memory of him to fade from her mind, body, and soul.

Heart Body and Soul

Instant Recognition

Having just landed in Namibia, Zamora is tired and cranky but she must head straight to the FBI mock headquarters due to an untimely tie-up in customs. The car service delivers her and her luggage to the front door with only two minutes to spare, so slightly dragging she enters the offices and is directed straight to a conference room. A feeling of instant awareness hits both Zamora and Marquise at the same time. Zamora quickly scans the room to discover the reason for this feeling since she is sure she has never worked with any of the agents on this case before, and her eyes instantly collide with the eyes from her dreams as Marquise instantly looks in her direction. They both instantly register a look of shock on their faces before quickly masking their features before they are detected by anyone else in the room.

"Zamora," greets Head Agent Rick Price as he makes his way to the door, "Glad you could make it on such short notice." As he directs her to the only available chair which happens to be right next to Marquise, he states, "We were just about to begin the briefing." Introductions are made round the room before Rick gives the agents the details of why they are needed in Africa. Once the briefing is complete, Rick turns to Zamora and asks, "Have you had a chance to check into the hotel yet?"

"Unfortunately, no. There was a tie-up in customs when I landed, so I came straight here from the airport."

ReGina Crawford

"Well I'm sure one of the agents here can help you get to the hotel and settled in."

Before anyone else can respond, Marquise quickly speaks up, "I can get her squared away Rick since I believe that she will be occupying the room next to mine." He then looks her directly in the eyes, almost daring her to refuse his help.

Unbeknownst to Marquise, she is more than willing to let him assist her since she wants to know what the hell he is doing here on her assignment. "That sounds fine," she states more calmly than she feels.

The agents file out of the conference room on their way to the hotel, and Marquise spying her luggage picks up the cases as Zamora walks behind him sizing him up once again. Once he deposits her luggage in the trunk of his rental, he opens the door and assists her inside. He then jogs around the front of the vehicle and gets inside, before he can utter a word Zamora whispers fiercely, "What are you doing here?"

Marquise rolls his eyes and sighs before responding in an agitated voice, "The same thing you are doing here. I'm an agent on this case. When did you begin working for the agency?"

"I have been an agent for five years," she replies in an agitated voice of her own. "How do you go from being a small town sheriff to being an agent on this case in two years?"

Ignoring her question, he asks, "So you were with the agency the day we met on the highway?"

"Yes, and you were a small town sheriff," she responds with heat in her voice. "You still haven't answered my question."

Heart Body and Soul

Still ignoring her question, he asks another question of his own, "Why does a virgin FBI agent have sex with a man she meets on a highway in Georgia?"

"Why does a small town sheriff, who's obviously trying to become an FBI agent, have sex with a woman he meets on a highway in Georgia," she counters.

Running a hand over his head, Marquise takes a deep breath and exhales it slowly before glancing her direction, "Look we are not going to get anywhere by antagonizing each other. Why don't we get you checked into the hotel, and then discuss our situation?"

Taking a deep breath herself, Zamora looks directly at him as she replies, "I agree. I'm tired and hungry, and I'm not trying to be difficult. Seeing you in that room after what happened between us two years ago was just a little unsettling, that's all."

They continue the ride to the hotel in silence, as well as getting Zamora checked into the hotel. Once inside her room, Marquise orders room service while Zamora takes a hot shower. Once she is feeling refreshed and the food has arrived, they sit down to eat and continue their discussion. Since Marquise knows that she needs time to get adjusted to the new time zone, he begins to tell his story.

"I had already applied to the agency the day that we met on that highway on Georgia, and I didn't know that you were an agent. As a matter of fact, it took every ounce of control that I posses to not use my position as sheriff to not look you up these past two years even though you invaded my days and especially my nights during all this time. But I was determined to uphold the agreement that we made that day. It was that day, after you left, that I got the call that I was accepted into the agency. I got this assignment since I excelled in every area of my training and field work since accepting the position, and I had no idea that you would be assigned to this case as well. Believe me when I say that our being here together is purely coincidental."

"Okay, say I believe your story," Zamora begins. Undeterred by his raised eyebrow, she continues, "How do you suggest we handle being on this assignment together? I know you have to still feel the attraction between us, and I don't want it interfering with the job we were sent here to do."

"I suggest that we act like adults who can control their libidos, and do the job we are here to do. I really don't think it will be a problem since I doubt we'll be spending much time together other than at briefings."

"I hope you're right about that," she mumbles.

"Why is that," asks a curious Marquise.

"Because seeing you again is making me feel things that I haven't felt since the day we met," she responds looking him straight in the eye.

"Oh hell," states Marquise as he closes his eyes. When he opens them again, he finds Zamora still looking directly into them. "Are you telling me that I'm still the only man you've slept with?"

"What? Do you find that hard to believe," asks Zamora with more than a little indignation in her tone. "Did you think that because I slept with you that I would suddenly start sleeping around?"

"Hold on," begins Marquise while holding up his hands, "I wasn't implying anything. It's just that it's been two years and you responded to me so passionately . . .," he falters at the angry look on her face. "Look, I'm not trying to upset you, it's just that I kinda figured once you discovered passion that you would find someone else to explore it with."

"Well I haven't," she huffs. Then somewhat under her breath, she states, "No one has moved me the way that you do."

Heart Body and Soul

"I'm sorry, what was that?"

"Nothing," responds Zamora as she gets up from the table to walk over to the windows.

Marquise walks up behind her and wraps his arms around her waist, "Zamora," he whispers near her ear and feels the tremor of her body. He closes his eyes and inhales a deep breath, "Baby, I know this is hard for you, but it's hard for me too. I never thought I would see you again, but now that you are here with me I still want you. Maybe even more than I did before, since I haven't been able to get you out of my mind, out of my soul."

Unbeknownst to Marquise, Zamora has closed her eyes and is replaying the events of that day two years ago in her mind, and is having the same thoughts as Marquise. "I just wasn't expecting to see you again either, and seeing you is making me feel things I didn't think I would feel again," she states before turning in his arms. She looks into his eyes, and sees the same passion and desire in his eyes that she knows is showing in hers. "I don't know what to do with the feelings that I'm feeling. I've never been in a situation like this before."

"Damn," he mutters. "Please don't look at me like that. I'm already finding it hard not to take you to bed, and the fact that you want to be taken to bed is playing havoc on my senses." He feels more tremors from her at his words, "Aw hell," he states before he takes her mouth in an all consuming kiss. Zamora soaks up the kiss like the parched earth of Africa during the first rain of the rainy season. Consumed by the passion being transferred to her through the kiss, she moans and trembles in his arms. Once the need to breath becomes unable to ignore, Marquise releases her mouth and they both gulp in air as their hearts continue to beat at a frantic pace. Marquise rests his forehead against hers while he struggles to pull much needed air into his lungs, but her trembling gets the best of him and he goes for her mouth once again. Unable to resist the magnetic pull of his mouth, Zamora responds with a desperation of her own as she returns the kiss.

Unable to hold out any longer, Marquise picks her up and carries her to the bedroom and lays her on the bed. Just like two years ago, they are both so consumed by the passion flowing between them that nothing else matters. He systematically undresses her as well as himself only taking his lips from her body to remove her shirt and his. Once he has her naked before him, he can't resist the urge to taste her core and so he does causing Zamora to bite her fist to keep from being heard back in the states. As her hips jump off the bed, he places his palm on her stomach to ease them back to the bed so that he may enjoy the feast he's been craving for two years. His moans of ecstasy mingle with hers as he savors the taste of her, and he doesn't let up even when her orgasm crashes over her causing her to lift her hips off the bed once again.

Content that her taste is deeply embedded within his taste buds, he reaches for his pants to retrieve a condom and sheath himself before moving between her parted thighs to give her the ride of her life. The initial entry causes both of them to moan from the sensations it sends cascading through their bodies. Marquise pauses as he tries to regain some semblance of control over his heart, body and soul, but Zamora wants none of that and squeezes him with her internal muscles. Unable to hold back, Marquise strokes her at a hard grueling pace that has them both climaxing in no time at all. He muffles his growl in the space between her neck and shoulder, while she places her fist in her mouth to keep from screaming her joy. It takes them both a while to recover enough to move let alone speak.

"Baby, are you alright," asks Marquise as he rolls to his side a few minutes later.

"Mmmm. I've never been better," is Zamora's response as she places fleeting kisses across his chest.

Heart Body and Soul

"You keep that up, and there will be a second act to this play." Zamora responds by circling her tongue around his nipple before covering it with her mouth and sucking. "Oh shit," is Marquise's response, and Zamora moves to his other nipple. "You know you're pouring gasoline on an already blazing fire, right," asks Marquise as sensation after sensation grips his body.

"Just trying to make sure the fire doesn't die down or go out," quips Zamora while still kissing and licking across his chest.

He flips to his back while pulling Zamora along to straddle his body, "There's no chance of this fire ever going out as long as you're around," he states as he places her silken sheath over his pulsating shaft. As she slides down further and further, Marquise moans and grips her hips in a firm hold. As she begins to rotate her hips in a circular motion, he begins thrusting upwards in an attempt to bury himself as far as he can within her womanly core. This round of loving is just as fast and furious as the first round as they try to make up for two years of doing without.